Assailants, Asphalt & Alibis

A CAMPER AND CRIMINALS COZY MYSTERY

Book Eight

BY

TONYA KAPPES

Assailants, Asphalt & Alibis

Abby pulled the pack off her back and got the journal out. She began to read, "At the branch head without crossing, then due east to the top of the ridge out of the clift country, then along the ridge to the right-hand side, and there will appear a place that is higher than the other. The hanging rock." Abby drew her eyes up from the paper and looked at the formation that appeared to hang over us from where we stood.

"The rock!" Queenie bounced on her toes and clapped her hands. "We've got to go up there."

"Let Mary Elizabeth tell us what's up there when she gets back." I covered my eyes from the sun. A couple of rocks tumbled down. "Mary Elizabeth? You okay?" I hollered up but didn't get a response.

The four of us stood there looking up as a few more pebbles fell.

"Do you think she's okay?" Abby gave me a worried look.

"We need to go up there according to the map, so let's just meet her up there." Queenie made a good point.

"Watch out!" Agnes yelled when a few larger rocks rolled down and fell into the water below.

The heat beat down over the rock, and when I looked at it, something shadowed the sun, as if there were a small eclipse.

"Avalanche!" I screamed and ran to the side, covering my head with my arms before I knocked Agnes out of the way with my body.

I heard a loud splash into the water—then silence.

I gulped and looked up. Mary Elizabeth stood on the hanging rock above the branch and waved.

"All done!" She grinned, having no idea what just happened to us down here.

"Is everyone okay?" I asked and made sure to look at them. They all looked okay. "Did you know big rocks fell like that?" I asked them since this was my first time here.

"It wasn't a rock," Abby said, her voice cracking.

We all looked over to where she pointed.

"My pearls!" Mary Elizabeth screamed from above.

Mason Cavanaugh lay face up, eyes open, floating in the water, with Mary Elizabeth's pearls in the grip of his hand.

"The curse." Agnes's words sent chills along my spine.

Author's Note:

This particular fictional installment of A Camper and Criminals Cozy Mystery was taken from a legend or tall tale told to me growing up.

The true story of the John Swift Silver Mine is one of the oldest legends of Kentucky recorded. It has been passed down through generations and was told to me as a child, and I told it to my children.

According to the legend, John Swift came to the Daniel Boone into Kentucky in the 1760s on a mining expedition. He came across a wounded bear. John Swift claimed the bear led him to a vein of silver ore in a nearby cave. For the next nine years John Swift continued to mine that cave, where he carried out silver bars and minted coins. He also claimed in his journals that he buried vast amounts of the fortune in various locations throughout the forest.

When you think of ginseng, do you think of Kentucky? Well… ginseng is a high commodity in the Daniel Boone National Forest. So much so that you have to obtain a harvester permit to pick and sell the root. It's illegal to pick and sell. If caught, there's automatic jail time starting at six months and up as well as a huge fine. You have to be a licensed dealer in order to sell it from September first through December first in a calendar year.

You can't just harvest any ginseng plant you see. Taken from the Kentucky Agricultural website: *Plants must have at least 3 prongs with 5 leaflets on each prong. This is the minimum legal age. The market prefers roots that are 10 years and older. Any berries present must be planted within 50 feet of the harvested root with no tool other than your finger; the goal is to put the seeds in the soil just over half an inch deep.*
Like hunting season, there's a harvest season and buying season.

Note that any reference to the ginseng and John Swift legend was taken purely from the Kentucky Agricultural website and the Daniel Boone National Forest and Parks website.

As this book was written, there was a hold on any sort of harvesting ginseng or selling in the Daniel Boone National Forest, making it illegal, though people are doing it.

I knew both of these concepts were awesome things to put in a book. Of course, all my book is fictional but loosely based around the John Swift legend and the ginseng issues. And I knew the Laundry Club ladies would love to be on the trail of a good treasure hunt.

So I hope you enjoy a little bit of Kentucky history from our famous John Swift legend as much as I loved incorporating all of it into this fun fictional series.

xoxo
T.

Dedication

I have to give a HUGE shout out to Author Sue Ann
Jaffarian! Sue Ann gave a generous donation

to a wonderful library to have her name in A Camper &
Criminals Cozy Mystery Series book.

I'm beyond grateful for Sue Ann's generous donation and
happy to have create a character in

her honor. Hugs, Sue Ann!!! I hope you enjoy!

xoxo
T.

ONE

The silence from at least one hundred people was almost as deafening as the bullfrogs billowing around the Happy Trails Campground lake while one of the treasure hunters told the group about the regional legend of John Swift's silver mine.

The flicker of the red, yellow, and orange flames showed in all their eyes as they focused on the intriguing story of the possibility that in and around my campground could be a massive amount of silver just waiting to be claimed.

"In the year 1760, John Swift made his way into Kentucky from the Gap and followed the creek known now as Swift's Creek. He was a well-educated Englishman that was a natural-born leader and sailor of his own ships off the coast of the Carolinas. It was when he'd come to Kentucky when he met up with a man by the name of Montgomery. Swift wasn't happy with the British and let it be known. It was then he and Montgomery had begun to counterfeit the British crown as a way of getting back at the British for invading the land we are gathered upon today as well as the entire Daniel Boone National Forest." Mason Cavanaugh's voice held a mysterious tone that rose up and down with the importance of what he had to say.

He held up a piece of paper that appeared to be the journal he'd mentioned.

"Swift had heard of the mines in Kentucky and maybe a mention or two about there being silver here. Thus began his several mining expeditions to Kentucky." Mason leaned over his knees and swept his hands in front of him. His eyes grew big. The flames of the fire made his blue eyes sparkle to life, making the scene ominous.

"It wasn't until a wounded bear led a very courageous Swift to a rock house, which is what we call a cave. This was the first time Swift found silver. It wasn't the only rock house, or cave, where Swift found silver. He noted all of the places in his journal, including maps."

He held up more papers with upside-down V designs and big Xs scribbled all over them. He brought the paper up to his eyes and leaned into the glow of the campfire.

He read, "Taken directly from John Swift's journal." Then he continued, "*"Seven miles above the mouth of the creek is a natural rock bridge. On the northwest side of the creek, a short distance below the bridge, is a branch. Follow the branch to its head, thence ascend the ridge, leaving the highest part of the ridge on your right. Go along the ridge to a point that is higher than the others, where a large rock seems to have fallen from above. Go in between them. This is where we obtained our best ore."*

He pulled the papers down from his face and sat back, turning his head from side to side as if he were trying to see what others thought about his tale. His stare stopped on another camper. I watched as her brow rose and didn't break the eye contact.

He looked back down at his papers as if he were trying to compose himself.

"The creek he refers to we believe is what we know now as Swift Creek, located right here in Normal." He looked up, and a slow grin crossed his face. The flicker of the fire caught his eyes at the right moment, making shadows cross his face.

Goosebumps crawled along my legs.

"Don't tell me you are falling for this crap." Dottie Swaggert flicked the ash off her light cigarette and brought it to her mouth, taking a long draw. Her red hair lay in curls around her head. "Because if you do, I've got a gold mine right under my old camper over there. I'll let you have it for one hundred dollars." The smoke rolled out of her mouth, and she pointed to her camper at the front of the campground.

A few people turned around to shush her. She gave them the death stare with big eyes.

"All these people are fools." She took one last puff before she threw it on the ground and snuffed it out with the toe of her flip-flop. Dottie stormed off toward her camper. She'd had enough.

"Not all of those journeys were successful. Swift and his crew were met with numerous obstacles from Indian attacks to mutiny among his crew, which was when John Swift holed up in one of his silver mines and finished his journals. He even had time to fall in love with the widow Renfro before he was deported back to England, where he was convicted of counterfeiting the crowns. It's rumored he left his journals and treasure map with the widow Renfro

until he rejoined her after he'd served his sentence."
Mason's eyes shifted back and forth.

"Unfortunately, Swift became blind while imprisoned, making him unable to find his treasure, leaving it buried forever." He took a deep breath and sat up, pulling his shoulders ramrod straight. "Or until someone finds it."

Murmurs from the crowd around Mason came up as they dispersed to their own campfires, campers, or headed home. Abby Fawn, Queenie French, and Mary Elizabeth Moberly, my adoptive mother, all walked up. I glanced around them and noticed Mayor Courtney MacKenzie had made her way over to Mason.

Mayor MacKenzie rarely came to the campground for monthly themed parties, and her presence made me question why she was there. Mayor MacKenzie didn't do anything that didn't get her attention, and election year was right around the corner.

"Do you need any help cleaning before we go?" Abby asked, breaking my concentration.

"Nah." I blinked a couple of times to get present with my girlfriends. "It'll give me something to do tomorrow," I said.

Every month I hosted a get-together between the community and the camping tourists. It was a fun party where Blue Ethel and the Adolescent Farm Boys, a local band, strummed on their instruments, giving it their best go at bluegrass music while the guests enjoyed local foods donated by restaurants in Normal.

"That is a fun campfire story," I said to Abby Fawn, noticing all the camping lots and the campers I provided for rental were all occupied. It was nice to see all the campfire rings lit up. "I'm sure it's the talk around all the s'more-making." I noticed everyone was enjoying the ingredients I'd given them when they rolled into the campground as a little special treat to thank them for choosing Happy Trails Campground for their vacation.

"Story?" Abby swung her head toward me, flinging her ponytail around. She stared wordlessly at me.

"Oh, honey, it's no story." Queenie French's hot-pink Jazzercise leotard shimmered more than the blanket of stars in the midnight sky. She picked at the edges of her short blond hair nervously. "Don't you know all of these people are here just for the annual Legend of John Swift Excursion?"

"You're pulling my leg." Mary Elizabeth's southern-accented voice held questions. "Right?" She fingered the pearls around her neck.

"I ain't pulling nothing." Queenie's nose curled; her right brow rose. "I'm telling you, there's several people out there who have found crown catches from John Swift's counterfeiting in these here caves."

Mary Elizabeth ran her hands down her Lily Pulitzer jumpsuit and then clasped them in front of her.

"The library is filled with tourists trying to get their hands on one of John Swift's treasure maps." Abby shook her head. "I keep telling them they need to go to the Historical Society."

Abby was the local librarian, Tupperware representative, and social media expert.

"Is that why I've had an uptake in calls?" Queenie's face drew as she stepped to the side to get a good look at Abby. She put her hands on her hips. "I was about to tell the mayor I was stepping down as the Historical Society president because it's taken up too much time away from my Jazzercise classes."

Queenie French was in her sixties. She was active in the community and taught Jazzercise in the undercroft of the Normal Baptist Church. I'd like to say she kept all the citizens of Normal in shape, but she only kept them in the latest gossip.

"From now on, I'm telling them to go back to the library." Queenie crossed her arms in frustration.

"Or don't answer the phone." Mary Elizabeth's face lit up like it did when she heard Nordstrom's was having their big annual sale. "Abby, you don't need to worry about the library, because"—Mary Elizabeth bounced with excitement—"we are going to go on the expedition."

"Did you get into Bobby Ray's moonshine?" I asked, referring to my foster brother. "Bobby Ray!" I flailed my arms in the air and yelled over to him, where he was with a group of friends.

"Hush." Mary Elizabeth batted my arms out of the air. "I'm serious. We haven't done anything exciting since I moved here." She started to count on her fingers. "December, January..." She continued reciting the months. "Eight months I've been here and not been camping at all."

"In those eight months, you bought the Milkery and opened a bed and breakfast. I'd say you've been very busy." I recalled the dairy farm and all the hard work she and Dawn Gentry had put into the Milkery's old farmhouse to open a much-needed bed and breakfast in Normal. "Besides, I have to run the campground. Abby has to work at the library, and Queenie, she'd never cancel her Jazzercise classes."

"Yes, I would." Queenie nodded back and forth between me and Mary Elizabeth.

"I could take some time off too." Abby shrugged. "I have some vacation time. What are we talking, just the weekend?"

"Dottie said it's not real." A nervous laugh escaped me. I pushed a strand of my curly brown hair behind my ear.

I had to stop this nonsense. I'd seen that look in Mary Elizabeth's eye before, and it was the kind that meant when she had her mind on something, nothing stood in her way to get it, whatever it was.

"If you don't want to do it, then we will do it." Mary Elizabeth's chin lifted in the air, and she looked down her nose at me. "Though I'd normally beg you to wear something presentable, you're going to have to wear different shoes."

I knew when I'd decided to wear the cute sequined flats that Mary Elizabeth would love them. They were from the Neiman Marcus from my former life. A few of the finer things I did keep, and I pulled them out every once in a while. Plus, I loved how they sparkled and glistened like the lightning bugs when I was standing near the campfire.

"Oh come on, Mae." Abby nudged me. "It'll be fun. We can even drive your camper and stay in it instead of a tent."

"Sounds wonderful." Queenie did a grapevine dance move with excitement. "I'll be here in the morning." She waved goodbye to us and headed to the parking lot in the front of the campground.

"This is perfect." Mary Elizabeth squealed with delight, just like the time I'd agreed to enter the Miss Eastern Kentucky beauty pageant at the county fair when I was sixteen.

That turned out to be a disaster, and I'd put money on it that this little treasure hunt would be too.

The three of them had decided upon a time to meet in the morning. We all agreed I'd ask Mason if it was all right so we could be sure he didn't mind four tagalongs.

"I'll text you what he says," I told them.

"He can't stop us from going to look for the treasure." Queenie was bound and determined to go on the hunt this weekend. "I'm the one they have to register with, so I'll just march on over to the Historical Society office in the morning and put our names on the list. You just let me know which campsite they are intending to use."

"Campsite?" I asked. I was still a little green to most things in the camping world. "You mean campground."

"No. I'm talking primitive campsites, but you can put your RV on it, just not all the fancy you got here." She rolled her hand in front of her. "There are several campsites that cater to the treasure hunters just for the John Swift silver mine expeditions. Unfortunately, some of those roads are gravel and not stable for big recreation vehicles like your RV." She glanced over her shoulder to Mason's camper behind his big truck. "He must be going somewhere that's not too terribly hard to get to if he's taking that big thing."

"Either way, if he is, we can still go somewhere else." Abby smiled. "I have so many John Swift maps that I can get, it won't matter where we lay our heads at night."

"I'm still in." Mary Elizabeth rubbed her hands together.

She looked like she was in with her perfectly styled hair and beautiful red fingernails I was sure she'd just

gotten manicured by Helen Pyle down at Cute-icles.
However, I would be curious to see Mary Elizabeth without
her pearls, which I've never done. I swore she slept in
them.

"Fine. Y'all go on home, and I'll head on over to talk
to Mason." I shooed them off and made my way over to the
mayor and Mason's inner circle.

"Mighty fine party you hosted." The mayor flashed her
million-dollar pearly white smile that I knew had to come
from some dentist not in Normal.

It was one of the dye jobs only one of those sleep-in
dental plates could give, or so claimed the infomercials.
She had her long red hair pulled up in a high ponytail like a
cheerleader. Her long and lean frame wore a linen jumper
with a pair of sensible sandals.

"Thank you. Mason, I see you met our mayor." I
smiled, looking between them. "I'm so happy you're here."

"And miss a chance to talk to one of Normal's regular
John Swift hunters? Never," she gasped and drew her hand
up to her chest, showing off the hand with no wedding ring.
She batted those big eyes. In the dark of the night, I could
see Mason blush. "He's going to find that treasure, and
with his advice, I'm so pleased to let him know his

suggestion of the asphalt was presented at the Kentucky assembly, and I got it passed."

"You did?" Mason sounded a little shocked.

"What asphalt?" This was the first I'd heard of any projects taking place locally.

"As a matter of fact, they started a couple of days ago." She propped her hands on her hips in a bossy way. "I told them the sooner the better."

"What asphalt?" I asked a little louder this time.

"Last year the mayor had asked me what improvements she could make to the trails getting to the Swift mines, and I told her how we could stay longer, which does pour money into the community, if we had roads instead of gravel." He stomped his food in the gravel we were standing on.

If he only knew how much asphalt cost to replace the gravel, he'd appreciate that we let him even look for the John Swift, but I kept my mouth shut.

"I took his suggestion to heart and realized how right he was and saddened the treasure hadn't been found." She gave me a squinch-eyed look, like I better not have any sort of opinion on what she was yammering on about. "I went straight to Frankfort for the assembly when it was in session with my concerns, and don't you know they have grants for things such as this."

"As mayor, you didn't know that?" I just had a hard time keeping my mouth shut. But it was a very reasonable question.

"I have not only the Kentucky legislature and law to understand, Mae, but also the National Parks laws and regulations that have to go together." The mayor put her hands together like she was doing a puzzle with her fingers. "And it just so happens, they started on the gravel road to the Furnace." She raised her brows at me like I knew what the Furnace was.

"That's exactly where me and my crew are headed." Mason seemed very happy with the big news.

"Now, I did hear some rumblings from our local news reporter there was some whispering about some protesting going on from one of the environmental groups about asphalt." The mayor was quick to dismiss any sort of claims. "So just keep going tomorrow if anyone is protesting. I've got the police on alert."

I skimmed over her protest comment and decided to let Mason in on how me and my crew were going to join him.

"Mason, me and a few of my friends are going to join you if you don't mind." I looked Mason in the eyes and tried to determine what kind of man he really was and if he would help us.

"Ummm…" One of Mason's crew members let out a loud sort of protest before he cleared his throat and looked down at his feet.

"Your friends?" Mason looked up at me.

"Just me and a few of my close friends who have lived here all their lives, minus Mary Elizabeth, but she'll probably stay in the RV the entire time. Air conditioning and all." I waved my hand in front of my face.

"There's no electrical hookup at the campsite we are going to, so you probably wouldn't be comfortable if someone needs air." He looked as if he had an out with me.

"You know we are in the dog days of summer here." The mayor fanned her hand before her own face. "My mama never let me play in the creek during the dog days. Said it was bad luck. There are a lot of creeks near the Furnace."

"What is the Furnace?" I finally asked.

"It's a rock formation believed to be in the area where some of the silver is hidden. And with the new asphalt roads, there is a greater chance someone will finally find the silver after 400 years." The mayor was still selling the asphalt.

"You know, I think we'll be fine." I shrugged. "If not, we can leave."

"According to the Weather Channel, there seems to be a little rain moving in over the weekend but nothing to worry about." The mayor was saying anything just to keep in the conversation. She seemed a little nervous. "Maybe you and the gals should just hike your trails."

"I think we will be fine." I gave the mayor a hard look.

"If you really want to go." Mason gave in, but his friend stormed off. "We will be leaving from here around eight in the morning."

"Perfect. We will be ready. Have a good night's sleep." I walked away before he could stop and think about us tagging along, not giving him any time to tell me he really didn't want us to go.

"Mae! Mayyeee!" The mayor hollered after me and trotted up next to me. I continued to walk. "Don't you mess this up for Normal. You of all people know how important it is to continue with the great economy."

"What are you talking about?" I stopped and turned to look at her, a little confused. "Look at my campground. I obviously have the best in mind for Normal."

"You don't know, do you?" She smiled. "You know it's just a legend. The silver. I mean, John Swift is real, but it's been 400 years. No one has found it?" She laughed. Then she stopped when she saw that I'd not joined her. "You really believe the legend, don't you?"

"I never heard of the legend until tonight, but Abby and Queenie seem to believe it. We are really just going for the fun of it. Real or not." I shrugged.

"I don't care really what you think, but I'm going to do whatever it takes for everyone in the world to believe somewhere deep in the Daniel Boone National Park, specifically Normal, that the John Swift silver mine is still buried and ready for all the treasure hunters of the world to come here and spend as much money as they want in our town to find it. Do you and I have an understanding?" She cut her eyes at me and started laughing when Mason walked by. "I hope you girls have a great time. And good luck!"

I stood there watching the mayor sashay off to another group of campers to tout how she'd gotten the government grant for the asphalt.

"Some tale, right?" The woman I noticed had caught Mason's stare and almost threw him off his story stopped in front of me. "The John Swift legend," she clarified when she noticed my confusion.

"Oh, that." I laughed. "I had no idea. I've been here a while now and still don't know all the secrets the forest holds."

"There's so many secrets." She winked and headed off before I got to ask her name or question her any further. "Nice shoes, by the way."

Many more secrets? I stared at her since I was now more intrigued with the town I'd made my home. I clicked the heels of my shoes together and smiled.

"There's no place like home. There's no place like home." I laughed and headed in the opposite direction.

TWO

"I'm coming!" I hollered through my home on wheels from my bedroom, which was located in the far back.

My new home was a far cry from the Manhattan skyrise or the beautiful beach house in the Hamptons. You might question how on earth did I end up in the camper. Well, I'd say I wasn't the happiest person in the world when I found out my now-dead ex-husband Paul West, hence my last name, had pretty much screwed everyone we knew when he pulled one of the biggest Ponzi schemes that'd ever taken place in the United States. He left me with nothing but a run-down camper and campground along with a lot of people who, well, let's say had a very bad taste in their mouth about me.

I'm not going to lie. I'd planned on traveling to Kentucky, selling Happy Trails Campground along with the old camper, and getting back to my life in New York. Mary Elizabeth always told me nothing ever turned out as planned. Boy, was she right.

If you'd told me a year ago that I'd be living in a camper in the middle of the Daniel Boone National Forest in a campground that I owned and would have a dog and date a detective, I'd have laughed in your face.

Turned out, I was in love with my life in Normal, and I'd embraced my Kentucky roots once again. Again? Yep. I grew up in Kentucky. I loved my life until my family was killed in a home fire and I was placed into foster care.

Don't get me wrong. Mary Elizabeth Moberly's house was fine. It was all the manners and classes she insisted I take in order to be a Kentucky debutante that weren't so appealing. Now, if my mama had put me in those things, I probably would've loved them, but as a teenager, I didn't want no one but my mama. That included Mary Elizabeth.

When the clock struck midnight on my eighteenth birthday, I was outta there, and that's how I got to New York, where I'd become a flight attendant and met Paul West on a flight.

"Hey." I swung open the door, putting my foot in front of the opening so Fifi, my poodle, didn't run out when I let Detective Hank Sharp and Chester, his dog, into the camper. "No, Fifi."

Fifi danced around in anticipation of Chester. She loved Hank's hunting dog, though Hank didn't hunt. Darnell Grassel used to be Chester's owner. Darnell had died, and Hank took Chester in even though Darnell had family. Chester really took to Hank, so it was just natural he went to live with him.

"Do you two want to join me for a nightly walk?" Hank and Chester had come inside. He shut the door behind him and gave me a quick kiss.

"Of course we do. I'll go get my shoes." I headed back to the bedroom to exchange my flip-flops for tennis shoes.

It was pitch black at night here, without the glow of big-city lights. It was safer to wear shoes that covered your feet because we had plenty of snakes. They might not be poisonous, but nursing a snake bite wasn't on my to-do list.

I'd used every bit of space possible. I'd taken down all the walls and made it an open concept plan with the kitchen and family room in one big room. I'd put up shiplap walls painted white. I'd gotten a cute café table with two chairs from the Tough Nickel as well as a small leather couch. It was perfect for one. The floors were redone with a prefabricated grey wood. The kitchen cabinets and all the storage cabinets were white. I'd transformed the little camper into a country farmhouse.

I'd strung twinkle lights everywhere I could, and I redid the bathroom with a tile shower and upgraded toilet.

I grabbed my tennis shoes and sat down on my bed. It was actually very comfortable, and I'd made a headboard using some wooden pallets painted pink.

I'd gotten a dresser with four drawers from the Tough Nickel, located in downtown Normal, that went perfectly with my distressed look. The twinkle lights added a bit of romance, along with the fuzzy rugs and milk glass vases full of fresh flowers or wildflowers that grew here in the Daniel Boone National Park.

"What is all this?" Hank asked. "All this stuff on your counter?"

"I'm going on a treasure hunt." I tied up my laces. "I'm going with Abby, Queenie, and Mary Elizabeth to find John Swift's silver."

I headed back into the family room combination part of the RV.

"Oh geez." Hank ran his hand through his hair. "Did you really fall for all the gibberish from them?" He gestured to the outside.

I knew he was referring to the group of treasure hunters, including Mason, who were staying here for the night until they moved to the more primitive campsite, where we'd be going tomorrow.

"I think it sounds interesting and fun." I shrugged.

I grabbed the bottle of bug spray, which was a must when you lived in a campground or even just in the forest. Especially in the middle of summer, when the heat and humidity brought out all the bugs and creatures that loved to bite.

Hank had gotten Fifi's leash on her for me. Chester and Fifi were eagerly dancing in front of the door. They both ran around the campground freely during the day, but night was different. We had a lot of creatures that would eat the pups as a snack, and we didn't want that to happen.

"If I find the silver and cash it in, we'll be rich." I laughed and pumped the juice all over me. I handed the bottle to Hank when I finished spraying myself. "Besides, it'll be fun to get away for a couple nights."

"Couple nights?" Hank whined.

"Yeah." I put my hands together and batted my eyes. "Will you watch Fifi for me?"

I'd planned on asking Dottie to do it for me, but Fifi would much rather stay with Hank and Chester.

"I guess since I'm not investigating anything right now." Hank was a detective who used to be a Park Ranger part time. It wasn't until recently he'd become a full-time detective, and his office was located in the sheriff's department. "We can show her how the boys live."

Hank hadn't been living in the campground long. He had a trailer on his parents' property, but they had recently moved back from being mostly on the road with his sister, who'd been pursuing a modeling career that went nowhere.

Another story for another time. But the short of it was he lived in one of the rental campers from me. When I built Happy Trails back up, I'd fixed up some campers for people to rent so they could experience camping without having to haul their own. Happy Trails also had hookups for people who did trailer their own campers or RVs. The most popular were the small bungalows nestled in the far end of the campground in the woods. They were adorable and perfect for couples or friend getaways.

"You do know about the John Swift silver curse, right?" Hank asked on our way out of the camper.

Immediately Fifi darted to the right into the grass, the leash taut. Chester followed her, so that's the way we decided to start our walk.

"Curse?" I gulped, happy it was super dark and he couldn't see how big my eyes had grown.

I gripped Fifi's leash a little tighter. A curse? I'd not had a whole lot of luck while I'd lived in Normal. There'd been a couple of murders where I was somehow involved with finding the body or stumbled upon the killer. A curse was something I didn't need. No way. No how.

"Of course it's all part of the legend that a curse has been placed on treasure hunters, but over my life there's been a lot of people trying to hunt the silver. But it's silly." He whistled for Chester and tugged on his leash when Chester found something on the tires of Mason's big truck as we passed the camper he'd rented for the night.

"What about the curse?" I asked, not letting him off the hook.

"I recall Granny saying something about my granddad trying to find the silver." He was talking about Agnes Swift, his adorable eighty-something-year-old granny, who was still working as the dispatcher at the police station. "She said one of the guys with him had a heart attack while in what they thought was the cave with the silver where Swift had followed that wounded bear. That took a while to get him out. Another one of the men with him had tripped over a rock going into that same cave and broken his leg. After my granddad got him out, then my granddad got his truck stolen." Hank stopped and grabbed my hand, stopping me. "But that's all silly talk. Part of the legend."

"Hank Sharp," I scolded when I saw a little shimmer of entertainment on his face. "Are you trying to scare me into not going? Because I can ask Agnes, and she'll tell me."

"Tell you?" He let go of my hand and laughed. "She'd go with you."

"Then I just might ask her." My eyes narrowed to see what was rustling around in the bushes outside one treasure hunter's camper.

Hank and I both reeled the dogs in but not with a little protesting from Fifi. She was always determined to get her way. After all, she was a show dog before I had babysat her while her owner was in jail for one of those murders I'd referred to earlier. Fifi ran around this campground like a little floozy, getting pregnant by a bulldog named Rosco.

That's when she became my dog. The owner couldn't breed a tainted dog anymore, and Fifi wasn't considered a pedigree now that she'd ventured to the wrong side of the tracks, and the rest was history. From that point on, we were stuck together. She still roamed the campground, but I got her spayed just in case she got any more ideas.

"Who's there?" Hank bent down and pulled up the leg on his jeans, taking a gun from the ankle holster he wore when he wasn't working.

"Excuse me?" The man's voice came from beside the camper. "Who are you?" When he walked out of the shadow of the moon, I noticed it was one of Mason's guys.

"You're with the treasure hunters." I walked over to him. "I'm Mae. I own the campground. I thought everyone was asleep."

"Dirk Ivy." He rubbed his hands off on a greasy rag, put it in his back pocket, and extended his hand for me and Hank to shake. "Yep. I've been out here with Mason a time or two. He says we are getting closer."

"Me and my group of friends are going to tag along with your group." I got a chill when I noticed how he looked at me. "I guess it's okay."

"It's all good." Hank was obviously taking the opportunity to let it be known that not only was I his girlfriend, but he was a detective. "I'm sure these fine treasure hunters will keep you safe and sound since I'll be here making sure there's not anything to investigate." Hank put his arm around me. His gun dangled from his hand.

Dirk's eyes fixated on the gun, and he continued to watch Hank uncurl his arm and bend down to put the gun back in his ankle holster.

"I grew up around here, so you make sure you be careful," Hank warned. "I was just telling Mae about the curse."

Dirk laughed. There was almost what we called a shit-eatin' grin on his face.

"Part of the legend." He looked around his shoulder at the camper. "I guess the curse got my camper because I'm having to get a couple-hundred-dollar fix in the morning from your local mechanic before we even drive out of here."

"Joel Grassel?" I asked since Grassel's Gas Station was the only mechanic shop in Normal.

"Yep. I met his worker tonight. Bobby..." He searched his memory.

"Bobby Ray. That's my brother." I left out the foster thing because it didn't matter. I loved Bobby Ray Bond like a brother and truly tried to make up for the start in life he gave me when I ran off on my eighteenth birthday.

It was Bobby Ray who gave me the money. I never looked back, figuring it was the last time I was ever going to see him, until he showed up at Happy Trails Campground after he'd read an article about me in the *National Parks Magazine.*

That's when he came and brought Mary Elizabeth with him. My past had caught up to me. Something I thought I was for sure going to regret, but a few months into them being here had really been a blessing in disguise.

"He said he'd take a look at it in the morning when there's some light." Dirk shook his head. "Maybe it's the curse," he said with raised brows. "If that's all the curse does while we are here, we are good."

"Good luck." Hank nodded after he noticed Chester had his feel of Dirk's setup. "Do you know for sure where y'all are going to be setting up?"

Was Hank asking for me? Or was Hank asking so he knew exactly where we were going to be?

"Mason said he wanted to set up camp right outside of Ore, south of the Furnace." He rattled off places I'd never heard of, and I'd been living here awhile. "Mason wants to head north up to the rockhouse off the Furnace Creek where the West Mine juts off a little to the south."

"Is that right?" Hank seemed to be gnawing on the location. "I heard just last year they had closed down that path to the West Mine. Something about a mudslide."

"You'd have to ask Mason about that." Dirk shrugged. "He's the one who filed all the paperwork."

"Maybe we are going to take the new asphalt road all the way in." I was met with a look from both of them like I didn't know what I was talking about. "The mayor mentioned the asphalt was being poured in that area."

"Then I'm sure he's gone through the legal channels." Hank nodded before the gravel shuffled under his feet and we started back on our walk.

"See you in the morning." I waved at Dirk and followed Hank. "You didn't seem to like him too much."

"What on earth gave you that idea?" Hank asked.

"You asked him about the permit and all that when he clearly isn't in charge of it. Or?" I winked at him. "Are you worried about me being around these big treasure hunters and running off with them when we find all the silver?"

"Yep," he said in a stern, non-joking voice, "that's it. You got me."

"I'm kidding." I tucked my arm in his elbow and kept my thoughts to myself about how he was acting a little strange. "It'll be fun for me and the gals to get away."

"So it's only you, Queenie, Abby and Mary Elizabeth?" he asked, walking down the small pier that was right across the lake from my camper.

"Yep." I slipped my shoes off and sat on the edge of the pier. I unclipped Fifi and let her jump in for a late-night swim. Chester jumped in after her. I dangled my feet in the water and watched the goofy dogs in the glow of the moon. "I'm sure it'll be a whole lot of fun."

"Mmhmmm." Hank sat down next to me and reclined back on his hip, one leg cocked at the knee. He didn't put his feet in the water. "You really should ask Granny. She's on vacation this week."

"Really? You think she'd go?" I asked and put my hands on the deck behind me, reclining on them.

"Are you kidding? She loves this stuff. Anything to do with John Swift reminds her of my granddad." He pulled out his phone. "I'll even call her for you."

"You sure do really want her to go." I gave him the wonky eye to see exactly what he was up to.

"Fine. I want her to keep an eye out for your safety because the camp those guys are going to, it doesn't have a lick of cell service up there. If something does happen, you'd have to pack up and leave camp. Granny, she'll know exactly what to do." He was too busy dialing her number to see the sheer fright on my face.

I'd never been without cell phone service. Neither had the queen of social media, Abby. Queenie would be fine, and so would Mary Elizabeth.

What if there was really a curse? What would we do?

"She's really excited. I'm going to go get her in the morning for you." Hank looked a little more pleased. "What?"

"Nothing." I shrugged and whistled for Fifi, her signal to come.

"That look on your face doesn't look like nothing." His eyes narrowed when he looked at me.

"Do you really think there's a curse?" I asked.

"Now that Granny is going…" He gave me that southern, snarky smile I loved. "Nah. Y'all be just fine."

"Yeah. We will." I waved off any knots in my stomach and grabbed up Fifi when she swam next to the dock.

Hank and I laughed when both dogs did the shimmy shake, flinging water all over us, except the tone of my laugh was a little more nervous than Hank's.

THREE

The excitement over the prospect of finding the John Swift silver mine had me turning over a dozen times, wishing for daylight and wondering if we would have any luck. With the thoughts of what I could do with the money, the treasure was heavy on my mind. Before I knew it, I dropped off to sleep.

The smell of bacon was what really got me and Fifi out of the bed. I rolled over and pulled the curtain away from the window. Mason and Dirk were making breakfast over their campfire. The cast-iron skillet along with the tripod holder perfectly placed above the fire made me comfortable that they knew how to cook and showed their camping experience.

I'd learned over the past year that anyone could wing camping, but the true campers and hikers knew how to make a great meal over a campfire. Most used very few ingredients.

"Fifi, you're going to be a good girl for Hank and Chester," I said to her, throwing the covers off me. She bounced around like she knew exactly what I meant. She knew Hank and Chester's names, which made her crazy already, but staying with them would just top off her weekend. "Let's eat." I grabbed my phone off my dresser and turned off the alarm before it even rang and padded down the small RV hall into the kitchen, where I scooped some of Fifi's kibble into her bowl.

I quickly checked the time. Mary Elizabeth, Queenie, Abby, and Agnes would be here in about a half hour, which gave me enough time to grab a quick shower, get some of the specialty baskets from the front office, and pack up Fifi's things. Plus, I had to unhook, something I'd not done while I'd been living full time in the RV since moving to Normal. I had gotten a small car from Grassel's Garage that I drove around town when I needed to.

After my shower, I did a fast clean up, since the gals and I would make this our home the next couple of nights.

"Let's go see Dottie," I suggested to the dancing Fifi. She needed to go potty since she'd eaten all her food, and it would be a nice walk up to chat with Dottie about leaving her in charge, which I was completely fine with since she'd always been the manager even before I knew I owned the place.

Fifi had darted down the steps of the camper and was already running up the road toward the office.

"Mornin'!" I hollered to Mason when he threw a hand up. There was a scowl on Dirk's face.

Maybe he wasn't happy we were going to tag along. Maybe he wasn't happy how Hank treated him. Big deal. He was going to have to get happy because we were going, and nothing would stop us.

"Looks like a good weekend to go and chase a big lie." A puff of cigarette smoke poured out of Dottie's mouth.

"It's going to be a great weekend no matter what." I gave her a little shove on my way into the office. "You should come. Henry can watch the place for a couple of nights." I tried to entice her because Henry Bryan, my handyman for Happy Trails, was probably more qualified than either Dottie or me to run the place.

"Do you remember what happened last spring when I went chasing a money trail?" Dottie reminded me of a recent murder in Normal that I'd been trying hard to forget about since I happened to literally stumble on top of the body, bringing me nose to nose with the victim. "I'm done with tall tales. The only money I'm gonna chase is the paycheck you're going to give me for working double duty this weekend."

Fifi darted into the office and immediately planted her little self in front of Dottie's desk. Dottie had a bad habit of giving Fifi treats, and Fifi knew Dottie was a sucker for her.

"Fine." I held the door for her when I noticed her putting her cig out. "Keep an eye out for Fifi. Not that Hank won't take good care of her, but you know she can be a handful when she wants to swim with the ducks."

"We will all be just fine." Dottie's brow rose. She tossed a treat to Fifi and then walked over to the filing cabinet. She pulled open the bottom drawer and took out the most awful mess of wires all gummed up. "I can't let you head out to the Furnace without taking some walkie-talkies."

She handed the tangled mess to me.

"I have no clue how to use these." They dangled from my grip. "Do they work?"

"They might've seen better days, but they got me through a lot of storms over the years before we had all that fancy cell service in the campground. I wouldn't go to the

Furnace without them. There's not a bit of service up there, but I think the mayor has gotten someone to get some lines pulled once they get the asphalt roads poured." She walked back over to her desk.

Fifi was really showing off for Dottie to give her another treat. Fifi danced on her little back paws and did a circle, leaving Dottie in a fit of laughter. I put the walkie-talkie mess on my desk.

"You're such a good girl." Dottie continued to give her treats while I went over to the specialty baskets we offered the campground guests.

"I think I'll take a couple of the spa kits and a couple of the bath kits." I grabbed the few kits and shut the door behind me.

"You think y'all going on some spa weekend?" Dottie asked and laughed even harder at me than she did Fifi. "Mae West." She *tsk*ed. "This here Happy Trails is the Ritz Carrollton compared to where you're going."

I wasn't sure if she was trying to scare me or just keep me from going so she wasn't left out of the group, but no matter what she said, there was no way it could be that bad.

"I'm going to take my chances." I pointed to Fifi. "Be sure you take care of my baby," I told her and retrieved a grocery bag from underneath the coffee station stand so I could put the walkie-talkies in it.

"All right," Dottie said flatly. "If you don't make it back, who do you want to have Fifi?"

"Stop it." I bent down and rubbed my sweet little white fur ball. "You be a good girl for Mommy."

She licked my face and ran back over to Dottie.

"Huh." I pushed up to stand and got the items off my desk. "I see where I stand."

"We will be fine." Dottie looked out the window when a car passed. "It looks like Hank is back. Tell him Fifi is here with me and I'll bring her down later. She can keep me company."

"Sounds good. I'll see you in a couple of days," I said to her over my shoulder and gave Fifi one more glance before I headed out of the office.

In the distance, I could see Mary Elizabeth, Hank, Agnes, Queenie and Abby all standing outside of the camper in a little huddle.

Dirk was putting out the campfire, and Mason had already unhooked his camper.

"I'll be finished unhooking in a minute," I told the girls and gave Hank a quick kiss. Hank followed behind me, helping me unhook. "It only took a kiss?" I asked him and eyed the infamous blue bag… the potty bag he was handling.

"You just be safe." There was no joking in his tone. "I'm worried sick with you up there with no cell service, but Granny Agnes knows her way around."

"Why is everyone so worried about us?" I ran my hand down his arm. "Before I forget"—his worry made me remember Dottie—"Fifi is hanging out with Dottie today. Do you have to work?"

"I've got a few things we are investigating, so I'll be going to the office for a couple hours. I'll grab her on my way home." He smiled. "Anything you need me to do around here?"

"Nope." I shook my head. "Henry is going to clean up Mason and Dirk's spot before the weekend guests get here."

Our busiest times around here were Thursday through Saturday nights. The guests generally got here around Thursday night or Friday so they could have all weekend to hike and do what they wanted. We were completely full for the weekend.

"I heard over the weather alert this morning when I went into the office before I picked up Granny that there might be a few pop-ups over the weekend." He didn't tell me anything I didn't already expect. We were in the dog days of summer, which brought the heat and humidity along with a few showers here and there. Nothing like the tornadoes we have in the spring.

"Everything in the camper is secured." Abby had met us around the back side of my home on wheels as I took the stoppers out from underneath the rubber. "Agnes and Mary Elizabeth are on the couch with their seatbelts on, and Queenie insists she sits up front."

"Looks like you gals are ready." Hank put his hand on my back. "I'll get this taken care of." He still had the blue bag to deal with.

Hank gave me a quick kiss.

"Be careful," he warned.

"I will." I shook my head and tapped Abby because I heard Mason put his camper in gear. I looked over at him. We made eye contact and gave the good Baptist nod. "Let's go."

Hank stood there and watched as we got into the camper. Mason pulled out, then Dirk, and I followed.

I couldn't help but look in my side mirror at Hank standing there. Blue bag and all.

FOUR

There was a lot of excited chatter among the ladies as we made our way out of the comforts of Happy Trails Campground and hugged the curvy roads of the Daniel Boone National Park on our way to find the John Swift Silver Mines.

"You do know that my Graham and I did a little treasure hunting ourselves." Agnes Swift, Hank's granny on his mother's side, was as cute as a button. Not to mention feisty as a cat. "When Hank asked if I wanted to come along, I knew I had to get into my attic and get out Graham's old maps," she said. Then she dug down in her pocketbook until she pulled out a folded piece of yellowed paper.

I watched through the rearview mirror as she moved from the couch to the café table, where she put the paper down. I'd not yet told Mary Elizabeth there was no electric service where we were going.

Agnes's wrinkled hand smoothed out the map. Abby rested herself on her forearms and leaned over the table.

"I got the maps from the library too. One of them looks a lot like this one." Abby pushed off the table and bent down to retrieve the bag she always took with her to the library. She hoisted it up on the table, letting it land with a clunk. She took out all sorts of hardback books and a stack of papers. "I took every book ever written about John Swift, along with his journals."

"My Graham said those journals were so hard to read, and if we can decipher some of it, we just might find some of those crowns." Agnes nodded her head, running her hand through her grey hair before she pulled something else out of her purse. "Like this here." She tapped the paper. "'We first left between 25,000 and 30,000 dollars and crowns on a large creek running near a south course, close to the spot where we marked our names, Swift, Mundy, and one other name, on a tree with a compass and trowel.'"

"That could be any creek." Queenie swiveled her passenger captain's chair to turn completely around to face them. "I stopped and got the maps from the Historical Society, though I probably shouldn't've, but if I'm gonna find the silver this weekend, I'll give them a very hefty charitable donation."

Queenie also had a big bag full of papers and documents that appeared as old as Agnes's, and since I'd just learned of the John Swift legend less than twenty-four hours ago, I decided to keep my mouth shut on any sort of ideas I might've had—at least until I had some more information.

"Right here John writes in his journal." She called him by his first name as though they were on a first-name basis. "'Not far from these trees we left a prize near a forked white oak and about two feet underground and laid two long stones across it, marking several stone marks on the place.'" She thrust her head up and gave Abby and Agnes a good long stare. "Now, you two and I both know that can be anywhere in the entire Daniel Boone National Forest, not just here in this park."

"It sounds like you have a lot of hunting to do." Mary Elizabeth leaned over the couch and opened one of the kitchen drawers I used as the junk drawer. She rooted around in there until she took out a fingernail file and eased back onto the couch, filing her nails. "I'll be sure to have a nice supper fixed when y'all get back. That way"—she circled the file in a circle—"we all have a part when the treasure is found, and we can split it."

"Well, I declare." Agnes's saggy jowls dropped even more. "I never figured you to be a campfire cook."

"Campfire?" Mary Elizabeth fingered the pearls around her neck. "I'll be using that electric fire right there." She noted the small two-burner stove in my kitchenette.

"Electric?" Agnes shot a look at me in the rearview. "You do know there's no electrical hookup at the campsite, or any sort of hookup for that matter."

"What?" Mary Elizabeth shot up and moved to the edge of the couch, gripping the leather when I started to bring the RV to a stop.

Agnes and Abby had pulled the curtain away from the window to look outside and see what was going on while Queenie swiveled the chair to look out the windshield.

"Looky there at those kooks holding those signs. Don't they understand progress?" Agnes tsked. "Some do-gooder official from the environmental office probably sent them down here. It's all they've been talking about down at the station." She shook her head. "I'm so glad I'm off this week."

A line of protestors demanded the stop of the asphalt being laid down. They were chanting something, but I couldn't hear over the chatter in the RV about it. Everybody had a cause to chase after, and it wasn't my place to say whether they were right or wrong, as long as it didn't hurt my chances of getting at the silver.

Still, Mayor MacKenzie's little talk with me about saying anything about the legend not being real or even thinking it wasn't real was heavy on my mind. Here she was using up all this state grant money to fund a big asphalt road when there might not be any silver to be had. All the same, I was having a good time with the gals, and even the thought there could be something kept me going.

"This must be a doozy of a grant." Agnes unbuckled her seat belt and jumped up to get a look out the window over the top of the sink. "Because I just can't believe they'd go right through the ginseng fields."

"Ginseng?" I asked. "You mean the supplement or vitamin type ginseng?"

"Mmhhh." Agnes was about to rub a hole in my flooring, going back and forth between the two windows as the RV crept along at a snail's pace. "Didn't you know Kentucky ginseng is one of the most sought after by the

Japanese? That's why the national park has put a hold on any certified ginseng harvesting for the past couple of years." Her neck strained as she tried to see farther up the road. "The field over there is sparse too. I guess they're just gonna do without all the extra money that brings into the national park."

"Did you see in the paper where they arrested that one tourist for even picking any? He got a five-thousand-dollar fine and six months in jail," Abby told Agnes.

Agnes sat back down once we got past the protestors, the ginseng field, and the little bit of asphalt the workers had laid down. The gravel churned under the tires of the RV, smacking little pebbles up underneath the carriage.

"We gettin' close now." Queenie nodded and rubbed her hands together. "'Bout another half hour." Queenie wiggled her brows. Some sort of body part on Queenie was always wiggling and jiggling, which made her perfect as a Jazzercise instructor. "Girls, you better get a little shut-eye because once we get there, I'm hittin' the trails."

I had no clue where we were going, but following right behind Mason and Dirk was where I was going to stay.

They all must've taken Queenie's advice because when I looked back to see what happened, it got suddenly quiet.

All of them had their heads thrown back, eyes closed, and appeared to be what Mary Elizabeth would call resting their eyes.

After about fifteen minutes of gravel road, we turned down a dirt road for another fifteen miles before I saw a sign that read JOHN SWIFT SILVER MINE CAMPGROUND written in black paint on a piece of wood stuck in the ground. The dirt road just stopped, and we continued on the grass until it opened up to a clearing.

A few tents were already set up near the far end of the space where the tree line had shaded a few feet. A small cabin-type structure sat in the middle with a permanent campfire structure enclosed with cement blocks.

"Lordy be, if Ritchie Stinnett don't look bad." Agnes got out of her seat belt again and propped herself up between the two captain chairs, looking out the windshield. "I ain't seen that boy since he was knee high to a June bug." Her chin jutted forward as her eyes squinted. "Look at that tangled mess of hair he's got."

The pimply-faced young man had patches of beard that his razor had obviously missed. He wore a T-shirt that used to be white but was covered with dirt spots. His long pair of cut-off shorts showed off his scrawny legs. He had on a pair of brown hiking boots. He flailed his arms in the air and pointed our RVs to the far right of the clearing.

I threaded the RV through the people who didn't seem to care that this big recreational vehicle was coming toward them. They continued to look at their maps.

"I really don't see any hookups." Mary Elizabeth pressed her lips together as tight as a zipper and breathed all hot and heavy, giving off her disapproval.

"Did you think I was a liar? Or a jokester?" Agnes's head jerked to look over her shoulder at Mary Elizabeth. "There's no electric, no water, and no cell service."

"What on earth am I going to do without air-conditioning?" Mary Elizabeth threw one hand over her mouth and the other to finger the pearls around her neck. "I mean sleeping and all?"

"We will just have to rely on the open windows." Abby got up and started to open the windows as the RV came to a stop where Ritchie had parked us, like those workers at the airport pull the planes to the ramps.

"That just won't do." Mary Elizabeth grabbed one of Agnes's maps off the café table and started fanning herself.

"Have you lost your ever-lovin' mind?" Agnes jerked the paper from Mary Elizabeth. "My Graham went through a lot of trouble working on these, and I've gone through just as much effort preserving them. Do you want to split this treasure or not?" Agnes wagged a finger at Mary Elizabeth. "Because if you do, you're gonna have to take off them pearls and get dirt under those fancy nails."

I tried not to look back at Mary Elizabeth, though I could only imagine the look on her face.

FIVE

"I hope them protestors didn't cause y'all too much trouble." Ritchie Stinnett had already planted himself at the door of the RV, his hand out. "How many of y'all in there?" He craned his neck to see in the door.

"Five of us." I didn't even bother saying anything about the protestors because he'd already moved on.

"It'll be fifty dollars a night. Ten each," he said and grabbed everyone's money as they anted up their part.

"Is there really no electric?" Mary Elizabeth held on to the edge of her money.

"No'm, there ain't. But you gonna be too busy looking for the silver to worry about any sort of electric. You gonna be so plumb tuckered out, you won't be able to get them fancy pearls off your neck to sleep." Ritchie Stinnett smiled, which didn't do much for the poor boy's looks. His teeth were rotted.

"Oh dear." Mary Elizabeth backed into the RV, her hinny leading the way. "I wonder if you could call Hank to come get me."

"There's no cell service." I pointed to my phone, sitting in the cupholder of the console up front between the captain chairs. "Go on and look."

She was bound and determined to prove me wrong.

"I'm gonna take my Metamucil before we get going." Agnes and the others got out of their seatbelts while I headed out the door to greet Ritchie and get the layout of the land. "Where you going?"

"You can't go without us." Queenie dug through her overnight back.

"I'm just going to see what I need to do with the RV and find out from Mason what our plan is." I sighed deeply, wondering exactly what I'd gotten myself into.

The heat hit me, taking my breath as soon as I'd opened the door. It would just be a matter of seconds before Mary Elizabeth had her first conniption about the heat and demanded something be done.

Ritchie had walked over to Mason and Dirk to collect their money, so I headed on over to talk to them and really get a handle on how all things treasure hunting happened.

"I'm serious, Ritchie," said Mason. "I've been here a long time, and if it doesn't get straightened out"—Mason pointed to me—"we will take our money back and head on out. There's plenty of camps around here. In fact"—Mason rocked back on the heels of his hiking boots—"Edward Summers had sent me an email saying the new asphalt had already let him get internet into his camp. I could do a lot of research with the internet at night when I'm not hunting, so just go on and give us all our money back."

"Now hold up," Ritchie stammered. "I can't help who shows up here without a reservation. Can't you just go on your way and she go hers?"

"Who?" I asked, wondering if they were talking about me.

"Sue Ann." Mason nodded toward the other camp we'd seen on our way in.

"Sue Ann?" I asked and glanced over when I noticed the woman stalking over to us. The closer she got, the more I recognized her as the woman who was at the campfire.

The one who told me the forest held more secrets than I was aware.

"Sue Ann Jaffarian." Mason's scowl told me how he felt about her. His mouth twisted. "I'm not going to try and make nice after she stole my maps."

"What is going on here?" The woman planted her hands on the waist of her too-short shorts. Blond curls framed her bright, Cupid-like face. Perspiration oozed out from underneath her makeup as words poured out of her mouth. "Are you still stuck on the fact that I know something or two about the John Swift silver and don't have to rely on you?"

"Rely on me?" An evil laughter escaped Mason. "You took it all. Little floozy."

"What did you say?" Sue Ann snapped, showing off a little of her spirit.

Mason looked at her with a wide grin on his face like he knew he'd just poked the bear.

"You heard me. Jezebel." Mason's jaw tensed.

"You are a crooked, lyin' son of a..." She looked at me then zipped her lips. "You know what you are." She swerved then quickly turned back around with a closed fist and gave him a swift knock to that tense jaw.

Mason's head swung to the side. He brought his hand up to where she'd landed the blow and rotated his jaw both ways as though he were working out the pain he was trying to hide.

"I oughta," he said through gritted teeth.

"Oughta what?" Sue Ann tugged the edges of her T-shirt over the waist of those too-short shorts.

"Now, now." Ritchie pushed between them. When I got a good look at him up close, Agnes was right. Though I'd never seen him before, he was a scrawny and pale fellow. Kinda sorry-looking guy who probably worked hard just to make a buck. "Can't we compromise here?"

"Why not now, Ritchie?" Sue Ann stuck her hip out and planted a fist on her hip. The other hand she fisted and stuck in the air, shaking it at Mason. "You better wipe that smug look off your face, or I'm gonna get the other side."

"Violence is not good around here." Ritchie seemed to have taken Mason's side, for which I could not blame him. "The trails and hiking around here is very dangerous in the calmest of situations. I can't have the two of you taking your lovers' spat out there and risk getting hurt."

"Lovers' spat?" My brows rose a notch. "You two?"

"No." Mason spit on the ground, nearly getting Sue Ann's boot, making her jump as if a rattler was underfoot.

"Fine." She threw her hands up in the air. "But you." She pointed straight at Ritchie. "I'll never do business with you again." Then she swung her finger at Mason. "I do hope the curse of John Swift gets you while you are here."

"Curse, my butt." Mason shook his head and rolled his eyes. "Good riddance, thief!" he called out to her with a big smile on his face, even though he rubbed his jaw where she'd socked him.

Ritchie gave each of us a hard look before he walked away.

"What was that all about?" I questioned Mason.

"She's my ex. We did a lot of treasure hunting together. We broke up, and I found out about her stealing. Some of my very own maps I'd made from years of research were gone. Luckily, Dirk has a great memory, so we were able to get some of the points back on a new map."

"Did you ask her about returning them? Or calling the police?" It seemed like a logical thing to do when you were accusing someone of stealing something so valuable from you.

"Are you kidding? A map for a 400-year-old treasure that most people think isn't real?" He made a good point. "The police would laugh at me."

I was going to encourage him to rethink that, but Hank's voice started playing in my head on how it wasn't real, and then there was the matter of the mayor and her veiled threat toward me to keep my thoughts to myself.

"I'm not saying we have the solution, but three of my five have their own maps. Agnes, the older lady, her husband hunted for the silver for years, and she brought his maps." I saw the spark in Mason's eye come back.

The roar of Sue Ann Jaffarian's RV and her crew revved up. Mason's spark dulled.

"I'd like to look at those maps." Mason turned back to me and stared intently like he was trying not to look Sue Ann's way.

The door of my RV swung open. As if on cue, Mary Elizabeth came out, in sweat and all her glory. She hemmed and hawed down the steps and over to us.

"Or look at those pearls." Mason's eyes grew big.

"Hi, darlin'." Mary Elizabeth fanned her face. "I swear, hon, you're gonna have to call Hank and get me out of here before I melt."

"Yes'm." Mason smiled. "My mama used to say back in Georgia that this heat is for training ground below."

"Below?" Mary Elizabeth drew back and lifted her hands in the air. "I don't dare plan on going down below." She gestured to the heavens. "That's why I can't take this no more."

"Tell me about those pearls." Mason was stuck on those silly little round cream-colored balls lying around Mary Elizabeth's neck.

"They were my great-grandmother's. They came from the Wilsons' wealth down in Western Kentucky." She talked as though everyone on God's green earth knew about the Wilsons and their wealth. "They've been in the family all this time, and I had adopted Maybelline here in hopes she'd one day respect them."

"You two?" Mason wagged a finger between us. "You can't be her mama. Sister maybe."

Hold the horses! Was Mason flirting with Mary Elizabeth?

"Oh, you." Mary Elizabeth blushed like a summer wine. She stood up a little straighter and shook with laughter. "Why, I didn't birth her." Mary Elizabeth ran her hand down her Lily Pulitzer blouse.

Now she was denying me? I sucked in an audible deep breath.

"I wanted a girl so bad that I couldn't resist that cute little face when the state needed her to be adopted." Mary Elizabeth grabbed my chin and gave it a good shake. "She's a doll and single."

"Mary Elizabeth!" I gasped. "No." I shook my head. "I'm not single. I'm dating. Hank." I flipped my hand back and forth. "You met Hank. Remember Hank?" I gave Mary Elizabeth the wonky eye.

"I don't see a ring. Do you, Mary Elizabeth?" Mason smiled and winked. I wasn't sure who he winked at, but he made Mary Elizabeth go weak in the knees.

"It's the heat, hon." She smiled, making me unsure she didn't pretend to get all side-ogling the way she acted as he helped steady her.

"I sure would like to give you a pretty penny for those pearls." He was so close to her neck that I thought he was going to kiss her.

"You don't have enough money to burn a wet mule, much less give me even half the cash of what these pearls cost." Mary Elizabeth just gave him her version of the southern "God bless you" without even having to say it, making me happy to hear that she wasn't being fooled by his flirting ways.

"I might have a couple of cents if you'd just let me touch them and see if I can give you a good price?" Mason was like a booger on a finger. He wasn't about to be thumped off. He was even brave enough to put his hand out, extending it toward the strand of pearls before Mary Elizabeth smacked it away.

"It doesn't seem like you're too popular with the ladies today." I laughed. "Mary Elizabeth, you need to go on in the RV and let the air conditioning cool you down until we decide what time we are hiking out today."

"Are you sure we can't get ahold of Hank somehow?" Mary Elizabeth wasn't listening. This was what made me so angry when I was a teenager and caused me to run off on my eighteenth birthday.

"You can do two nights." I took an adult stand. "I'll be in there in a minute. I want to talk to Mason."

At least he was taking note and being good, not bothering Mary Elizabeth about those pearls.

"I'm hungry." She stomped off like it was her decision that made her leave and not me telling her to go back. Whatever it took.

Mason and I stood there watching her head back to the RV. Abby, Queenie, and Agnes all stared at us from the various windows.

"She's a feisty one." Mason joked and took my attention. "I have to apologize for my reaction to Sue Ann, but she and I'd been together for over ten years. It was time to separate, but when I found out…" He shook his head, disappointment in his tone. "I was heartbroken. To think if she finds the John Swift silver before I do. That would be a kick in the teeth."

"No big deal." I waved it off. I might not have agreed with how the two of them handled things, but it wasn't my battle to fight, so I just left it as it was. "She is gone now."

"I hope so. I wouldn't be surprised if she were to show up while we are out there, now that she knows we are here." He looked over his right shoulder into the woods. "There's more ways than one to skin a cat. Just like you said about the three different maps your friends have."

"What time are we heading out?" I asked. "I can see if we have time to take a look at all our maps."

I wasn't about to give him our maps if he wasn't willing to show us his.

"You're serious?" His brows furrowed.

"Serious?" I didn't know what he was talking about.

"Serious about finding the treasure?" He snickered. I didn't like how he was acting toward me, like he'd treated Sue Ann.

"Why in the world would I be here in the dog days of summer if I wasn't? Or dragging them along with me?" I asked and tried to read his facial features.

"I was thinking the five of you thought it was an entertaining tale from last night's campfire." He was really full of himself. I almost wished Sue Ann was still here to give him another piece of her mind. "Now that I can see you're serious, I guess you should know we will have a meeting before campfire supper tonight, get a good night's sleep and head back out in the morning."

Dirk had walked up and planted himself just a little behind Mason.

"We aren't going tonight?" It seemed like a big waste of a chunk of daylight and time.

"Listen." He leaned in a little closer. "Leave the planning up to me. I've been doing this for over fifteen years. Each year I get closer and closer. There's no good that comes from being hasty. This is how I've always done it."

He looked over his shoulder at Dirk, and Dirk nodded to confirm.

"I'm going to get the meeting papers ready now that Dirk has set up the shelter tent." He was referring to a large white yurt that was set up between Dirk's RV and Mason's camper, which was now unhooked from his truck.

Dirk had muscled all the equipment without any help.

"He's a tough one." Dirk waited until Mason was out of earshot. "Hey, thanks to your brother for fixing my camper."

"Yeah. No problem. He's really a great guy, and you can tell Mary Elizabeth that because she's proud of him." I gestured to my camper. "She's in there all hot."

"She'll be okay once the low pressure comes through. If it does rain, it might take out some of the humidity." He checked his phone. "According to the weather update, it might rain a little more than initially thought. But we have enough equipment to get done what we need done."

"I don't understand why we aren't looking now. We are burning up daylight." I shrugged.

"It's Mason's way." Dirk shrugged. "I don't agree with him, but he seems to think it's the best, and once I'm boss, I can do what I want to."

The little strain in his voice made me question just how long Dirk wouldn't be the boss.

"Until then, we will have to do what Mason suggests." Dirk glanced around to see the commotion behind us. It was Mason carrying long rolled-up white sheets that looked like those building plans out of his camper and heading into the yurt. "I suggest you and the ladies take a nap because starting in the morning, it's all go until we pull out of here on Sunday."

I couldn't really do anything but listen to Dirk and Mason. Could I?

SIX

"Wait and see." Agnes snatched up her maps and grabbed the backpack she'd filled with all sorts of things while I was outside with Mason. "You think I'm wasting my Graham's maps and daylight to wait for some amateur treasure hunter? You got another thing coming."

"He said that…"

I was interrupted by Queenie. "Who cares what he said?" Queenie strapped on her hot-pink fanny pack. She unzipped it and filled it with some granola bars. "We paid Ritchie our fee, and I'm going to use it up. Even if just for the exercise since I didn't get to teach my Jazzercise class today."

"You really think we should?" Abby was the only one who had some sense in her.

"I'm going." Mary Elizabeth emerged from the bathroom. She'd completely changed her clothing into a pair of jogger shorts and T-shirt, minus the pearls. My jaw dropped. "What?" She lifted her chin in the air and looked down her nose at me. "I wear this when I'm cleaning the bed and breakfast."

"But your pearls?" I questioned with a little shocked tone. "I don't think I've ever seen you without them around your neck." I really dug deep in my memory and could never recall a time.

"There's no way I'm going out there with those precious family jewels on and risk a tree limb snagging on them or something unthinkable happening." She lifted her hand to where the strand had lain and rubbed. "If we are going, I think we should go."

"All in favor of going now for a few hours, raise your hand," I said.

"What? Are we five years old?" Queenie asked sarcastically and raised her hand along with Agnes and Mary Elizabeth.

Abby and I looked at each other. My eyes grew big, gesturing for her to say something about why she didn't think it was a good idea.

"I think we should listen to…" Abby was barely audible.

"Three against two. We win." Agnes pointed to the three of them, a side of her I had no idea existed.

"I knew you were feisty but had no clue you were so passionate about finding silver." Abby laughed and grabbed the backpack she'd brought.

"Before we head out…" I stopped them before they opened the door. "Don't we want to know whose map we are looking at first?"

"Hhmmm…" Queenie's mouth twisted six ways to Sunday as she thought about it before she said, "That ought not to be a bad idea."

"We have three maps, right?" Mary Elizabeth was good in this sort of take-charge situations. "Abby's library copy, Queenie's Historical Society copies, and Agnes's 'my Graham's' copies."

I tried not to smile when Mary Elizabeth referred to Agnes's husband the way Agnes always referred to him.

"Sounds about right to me." Agnes gave a hard nod.

"We are here tonight, Saturday, and Sunday." I could see where Mary Elizabeth was going with this. "Leaving Sunday night."

"No wonder where Mae got her smarts." Queenie tapped her noggin. "One map a day. But whose map is going to get the shorter time today?"

"We can do mine," Abby suggested. "It's not like I'm as invested as the two of you seem to be with yours. It's also the most public one, and if no one has found the treasure using it yet, then it might be good not to spend so much time on it."

"All in favor?" Queenie took my line.

All of us raised our hands.

"Let's get going," Agnes said and bolted out the door before anyone could protest anything else.

The five of us stood outside the camper. Mason and Dirk were hunched over a table in the tent. Mason was pointing to something, and Dirk shook his head in protest.

"This is ridiculous!" Dirk ran his forearm down part of the table, shoving off papers onto the ground.

"You're a fool!" Mason grabbed Dirk by the arm. "When you're in charge, you can do what you want. But for now, we are doing it my way."

Dirk jerked his arm away from Mason. Mason brought his hands up to his face in a boxing position like the two of them were going to go at it.

"I'll be in charge sooner than you think!" Dirk jerked around. When he saw the five of us standing there with our mouths practically trying to catch flies, he sucked in a deep breath and composed himself. He took one last look at Mason before he stalked out of the tent.

"Ladies," he grunted and headed toward Ritchie's small cabin in the middle of the open field.

"Hey," Abby said meekly while the rest of us remained quiet and looked at him.

"Where are you off to?" Mason walked over, peeking out of the tent's open flap. He took a few seconds to look at each of us while I explained how we would just look at Abby's map and kill time by trying to find something on our own.

"It's better than sitting around being hot when I can at least be shaded in the forest." Mary Elizabeth had beads of sweat along her freshly waxed upper lip. "I'm a sweaty mess."

"No, honey." Queenie did some sort of side shuffle. "You are glistening."

Mason smiled, breaking the stern look he'd had on his face from the whole Dirk thing.

"You ladies be careful. Remember, John Swift encountered a few bears along the way." His eyes sparkled. You could tell he really enjoyed looking for the silver mines.

"If I didn't know better"—Mary Elizabeth shook a finger at Mason—"I'd think you were trying to scare us."

"Scare?" Mason gave her a shy smile and wink. "Me? Never," he gasped, and his eyes moved to her neck. "Oh my, your pearls."

"I took them off just in case I do see a bear." Mary Elizabeth was so good with comebacks that were witty. "Now, since you are cooking supper, please have it ready when we get back."

"Yes'm. You wait right here." He gave a soldier's salute before he disappeared back into his tent. He reemerged with some Ziploc bags in his hand. "Here's some food that will help sustain your energy while you're out there. You might think you aren't working your body hard, but you are."

"That's mighty kind of you." Mary Elizabeth took the Ziplocs and handed them to me as she turned her back, gesturing for me to put them in her backpack.

"I don't want to have to come out there and hunt for any of you," he told us in a voice of authority.

"We will be fine," I assured him and walked away with the gals following me.

"He sure has taken a shine to you." Agnes had taken charge and was the first one on the trail.

"He's just being friendly." Mary Elizabeth played it off.

All five of us were in a line as we walked what little trail was still trodden down from others. Just about half a mile into the hike, the trail was no longer visible. Agnes would stop a few seconds every hundred feet or so.

"Let me see here." Her little wrinkly hand held up the compass. She moved in a circle to find the exact direction she wanted to go. "My Graham said this was how people got lost. The trails stop, and people keep walking. My Graham said you have to use a compass." She eyed Abby. "You young people don't even know how to read a compass or map."

"Why are you lumping me into that mix?" Abby asked with an offended tone.

"Don't think I didn't notice you taking out your phone to see if you had service." Agnes' observation made us laugh. We were all guilty of trying to see if we were getting any sort of service. After I'd tried a couple of times, I just gave up.

"According to your map, Swift's first fifteen thousand crowns are twenty poles from the creek." She continued to look at her compass until she was satisfied with the direction. "That means we need to walk a little over half a mile before we get to the small rock near the blush-colored bush." Agnes made a karate chop move. "This way."

We all forged ahead, not questioning a bit of Agnes's ability to get us to the spot on Abby's map that led to a cache of crowns Swift had counterfeited while he was here in Kentucky.

The forest got thicker the deeper we went. I was happy to be in the very back because Agnes cleared some brush with her stick while Abby forged behind her. Queenie was next, and she whacked everything in her way, clearing the way for Mary Elizabeth, then me.

The sound of crackling leaves and sticks made me stop to listen. A few murmuring voices had me turning around to see who was behind me.

"Y'all," I whispered. The chills prickled the back of my neck. "Someone is out here."

Everybody stopped.

"Someone?" Agnes asked. "A lot of someones are here. All looking for the treasure."

Just as the words left her mouth, Sue Ann Jaffarian and a couple of crew members appeared from behind some trees.

I think they were just as shocked to see us as we were them.

"I'm so glad it's you." I put my hand up to my chest. The chills fell away. Then I started to explain myself. "Not that I know you, but I did see you back at Ritchie's campsite. And you never know who you'll see out here and if they are going to... kill you."

"Kill you?" Mary Elizabeth jerked back. Her brows furrowed.

"I'm just saying anything can happen in the woods." I had no idea why I kept talking. "Anyways, I'm Mae." I went down the line. "Sue Ann, this here is Mary Elizabeth, Queenie, Abby, and Agnes."

Sue Ann gave me a look as though I'd lost my mind.

"I can call you Sue Ann, right? I mean, I know we weren't introduced at the campsite, but Mason did tell me who you were, and I just..." I clamped my mouth together when I noticed her brows were digging, popping, and just plain confused with me.

"Yes. About that." She glanced over her shoulder at her crew members. She had a fistful of some greenery in her hand. "I'm sorry you had to witness that. He just can't take it that I broke up with him, and I've got better people working for me as well as better at finding treasure." She gave a sly look to both the people with her. "He's spent the better part of the last six months trying to ruin my reputation, and I've about had it up to here with him." She took her finger and drew it across her neck.

I let out a little gasp from her gesture.

"We did get set up at another camp. Good luck on your hunt." Sue Ann shrugged as if what she said was A-okay.

"We have no idea what we are doing," Abby spoke up and took the map out of Agnes's hand.

"Speak for yourself, child." Agnes grabbed it back. "My Graham was a treasure hunter. God rest his soul."

"Did he have any luck?" Sue Ann actually sounded like she really cared.

"Close." Agnes wasn't about to say that Graham had failed at anything.

"Close but no cigar," one of Sue Ann's crew members said with a tone of sarcasm. Sue Ann nudged him, and Agnes glared at him.

"Is that his map?" she asked Agnes and gestured with her fistful of weeds.

"No. This is one from the library we are doing this afternoon just to get our feet wet in hunting. We are going to use my Graham's map tomorrow." Agnes had so much pride in her voice.

"That's wonderful. We are just hiking from the new campsite to get our surroundings since we don't want to have to waste any time tomorrow." She looked up at the trees. "It's nice in here. Shady."

"Why is it that you aren't hunting treasure now?" I asked because it was obviously something she and Mason shared opinions about.

"Once you start the hunt, you truly don't want to stop to go back to camp until the very last minute. As you can see, it's pretty dark in here with the sun beating down because the trees are so thick, they shade not only the heat but the light. When you set up camp, which takes a good half a day, it's hard to even go hunt and come back after a couple hours. You definitely don't want to set up in the forest because of all the creatures." She smiled.

"You mean the legend?" Mary Elizabeth quivered.

"Mason has you scared to death." Sue Ann laughed, and so did her crew. "Not the legend so much as the bears. Can we see your map? Maybe we can hike with you."

Agnes practically pushed all of us out of the way with her little eighty-year-old body so she could get to Sue Ann and show her the map.

"According to this map and Swift's April fifteen journal entry, he left fifteen thousand crowns about twenty poles that way." Agnes might not've gone treasure hunting with Graham, but she sure did sound like she knew what she was talking about. "There's a blush-colored bush next to a rock that's got three chop marks."

"I think we've seen that bush near the forked white oak," one of her crew members said.

"We don't know about this one. Also, according to his journal, he had two horse loads of treasure there." She smiled. "That's where we are going this weekend."

"You saw the bush?" Agnes asked with a lot of interest.

"We did a few months back. Remember, you're looking at a journal that was written in April. Springtime." She made a very good point. "With the seasons Kentucky has, a lot of those colors are turned green or even died all together."

It was like she took a big needle and popped a balloon. That's how quickly all of our bubbles burst with her words.

"Then we just need to go on back." Mary Elizabeth twirled around to where we'd come from.

"Hold on there." Agnes stomped her foot. "What kind of treasure hunter are y'all if you just hightail it back to the camp after a little, tiny setback?"

"Tiny setback?" Mary Elizabeth growled. "These journal entries are the only thing we have to go by, and that includes the colors of the bushes and trees."

"We still have the map. We still have the three-chop-mark rock. That won't change colors," Agnes spat back. "Now, you can go back by yourself, or you can go with us."

Sue Ann Jaffarian and her crew stood there as if we were a show to watch. They appeared to be entertained by the glee on our faces.

"Any words of advice?" I asked her.

"Okay, listen." Sue Ann took the chance to talk to us. "Treasure hunting is hard. If everyone doesn't like it, then one of you should head up to the information center back at camp."

"Information center at camp?" Mary Elizabeth really liked that suggestion.

"Yes. I'm sure Mason has a tent set up at camp already." We all nodded, and she continued, "In the tent is the information center. It's got all the maps and locations he and his team, which I think is just Dirk this time, will hike to and hunt around. They've spent years on these locations and have stacks of places to look. Each time we come out here, we pick one or two locations to hunt. Every day they'll come back and mark off places they believe where the Swift journals and maps have taken them. They will make notes about the places and log any sort of treasure they find."

"No one has found any sort of Swift mine." Queenie was very confident.

"Actually, several people have found a lot of the counterfeit crowns. We've found at least one every time we've come here to hunt. That's probably what keeps me coming back. It does make me feel like his claims are true." Her words got me a little excited to find something.

"Really?" I asked a little shocked.

"Are you not a believer, Mae?" she asked me. Apparently, I didn't have a good poker face. Something to remember.

A beeping sound came from the pocket of one of her crew members.

"You get cell service?" Abby Fawn jumped on it. She must've been having withdrawal from her social media.

"No. It's the walkie-talkie." Sue Ann stuck her hand out, and he gave her the unit. "Please tell me you have one with you."

All five of us looked at each other before we all felt ashamed and looked down at our feet.

"Go ahead," she spoke into the device.

"Yeah, Mason is at it again. This new campsite said they got a complaint, and we need to move." The voice on the other end came through very loud and clear.

"I swear." Sue Ann's face turned pink, but the more she talked, the more her blush turned to fire-engine red and dripped down her neck. "He's going to give me hives."

"What are we going to do?" one of them asked her.

"Kill him. He and I both can't be treasure hunters." She put the walkie-talkie back up to her mouth. "We are coming back. Don't do anything until I talk to them."

With that, Sue Ann Jaffarian and her crew headed back the way they'd come.

"What are we going to do?" Mary Elizabeth had the information center in her head now. There was no way she would let that go.

"I think we need to go back." I looked up and tried to gauge where the sun was located in the sky. In no way could I even see through the trees, but I did know it was getting darker, and soon what little light there was peeking through the leaves would be gone. "It's going to get too dark to find our way back."

"It's not the dark. I can do that with my compass. It's the bears." Agnes walked to the back of the line as I was holding up the rear. "My Graham said to never let a bear see ya in here. He said you'd never make it out alive."

Goosebumps ran up my legs. Was Graham talking about being attacked by the bear or by the John Swift curse?

SEVEN

The closer we got to camp, the more something just smelled better and better. When we made it out of the forest and back into the clearing, my stomach was delighted to see Mason had taken instructions from Mary Elizabeth about getting supper together.

Mason, Dirk, and Ritchie stood around the roaring campfire. There was a big pot hanging across the fire and a grill plate set up next to it.

"Y'all are just in time." Mason popped straight up from over the fire when he saw us walking toward him. "We are having steak nachos, grilling style."

My mouth watered at the sight of the steaks he had in the skillet. They smelled delicious, and the sound of the sizzle was music to my ears. I wasn't sure what it was about campfire food that made it taste extra good. Maybe it was the entire package of the sounds of the night or just being in the open air, or even among friends, but there was no place I'd rather be than right here watching Mason cook.

"Did you find anything?" Dirk was placing the tortilla chips in the large pot hanging over the fire. He added some black beans, corn, and green chilis along with some shredded cheese.

Queenie, Abby, and Agnes had walked over to the cooler to get drinks.

"A whole lot of Sue Ann," Mary Elizabeth said, making Mason look over.

Dirk didn't stop layering the nacho ingredients on top of each other. He continued to look at the steak Mason was tending to, though he was Mason's sous-chef and getting all the food prepared and cooked at the same time.

"What she means"—I shot Mary Elizabeth a look—"is that we were hiking and ran into Sue Ann and a couple of her crew members."

"She was not happy with you." Agnes had joined us at the tail end of the conversation. "She said you keep getting her kicked out of campgrounds."

"You can't do that. The forest and park are open to anyone. Even the campgrounds." Queenie should have known since she was the president of the Historical Society. "Ritchie has to pay a fee, you know."

"Ritchie wanted to keep the peace." Mason flipped the steaks over. If I could've seen his face through the smoke from the steaks, I was sure he would look mad. It was the tone in his voice that told me he didn't like hearing we'd seen his ex. "Besides, he didn't kick her out."

He was taking up for Ritchie's actions as if Queenie were the camping police.

"What did she say exactly?" Mason took the skillet from the flame and put it on the rock next to us.

"She just said how the two of you dated and how you didn't want her here." I left out the part where she pulled her finger across her neck, wishing he were dead.

Not Agnes.

"She got word you had her removed from another campground, and she wished you dead." Agnes giggled. "You done made that girl mad."

"What's that saying about a woman scorned?" Dirk nudged Mason. They both laughed.

Dirk took the steaks out of the skillet and placed them on a cutting board, where he cut them into strips. Mason had abandoned the meal altogether and was visibly upset with the news about us seeing and talking to Sue Ann.

"She stole my maps. She doesn't deserve to be at this site." He jerked his hand towards the woods. "She thinks she can just come in here when I'm here and follow my maps. At least she can come when I'm not here."

Dirk looked at me from underneath his brows and rolled his eyes. He made me feel like this was an ongoing discussion between them.

"Did she honestly say she wished I was dead?" Mason's brows furrowed.

Mary Elizabeth dragged her finger across her neck, giving me an expression I didn't figure on.

"My pearls." She jumped up. "Now that I've been out there, I can say I participated in the John Swift silver treasure hunt. I can put on my pearls and stay behind tomorrow."

"Aren't you going to eat while it's hot?" Mason tried to stop her when he scooped up some of the layered nachos and topped them with the steak on a plate. "Those pearls can wait."

"I'm good." Mary Elizabeth hightailed it across camp to my camper. "I'll be right back."

Neither Agnes, Queenie, Abby, nor I needed any coaxing on having a plate. Just as we all sat down and got comfortable, the loudest shrieks came out of the camper followed by a frantic Mary Elizabeth.

"You stole my pearls!" she screamed to high heaven. "Where are they?"

"What? Who?" I put my plate down and walked to meet her.

"Him!" She continued to yell and point at Mason. "That sonofa…"

"Stop." I pushed her arm down. "What did you teach me about pointing at people? It's bad manners."

"It's bad manners to steal people's things." She spat and glared over my shoulder at Mason. "He took them, and I want them back."

"I didn't take anything." Mason's jaw dropped. He looked at everyone, put his plate down, and stood up. "I've been going over my maps and cooking. I didn't even go near your camper."

"You're the only one who even noticed my pearls, and we had a discussion." Mary Elizabeth stalked over to him and put her hand out. "You can give them to me, and we forget it, or I call Hank. Call Hank anyways, Mae."

Now she wanted to be bragging on me and Hank, but earlier, she was trying to get me all hooked up with Mason.

"We don't have cell service," Abby reminded her. She hadn't touched her food yet. She seemed to be waiting to see what was happening with the pearls. No way did this situation bother Queenie and Agnes. They were shoveling it in as fast as they could alongside Dirk.

"Let's go look one more time," I suggested, thinking it was a pretty good idea.

"Yeah. Maybe you don't remember where you put them." Mason had said the wrong thing.

"Are you calling me old? Are you saying my memory is gone? Because I remember fine how you offered me money for my pearls, and when I refused, you stole them when I turned my back." She rubbed her bare neck. "I knew I shouldn't've taken them off."

"Just go back and look for them. Make sure before you go accusing someone," Agnes grumbled.

Mary Elizabeth let out a few huffs and puffs before she gave in to all those who agreed.

"It's not like he's going anywhere," I told her while I escorted her back to the camper. "Maybe they fell out of wherever you put them. It's not going to take us long to find them."

"I'm telling you I didn't misplace them, or they didn't fall out. I looked before I realized they were gone and came out here to get them back from Mason." Mary Elizabeth was getting older, though I didn't think she was getting Alzheimer's or anything. Just forgetful.

"I forget things all the time," I confessed. "Like keys." I shrugged.

"Are you really going to try to sell that to me? Because I'm not buying." She stomped up the step into the camper. We walked back into the bedroom. "I put them right here in the red velvet pouch after I changed my clothes. The red velvet pouch they came in, and it's gone."

"Let's just look." I took the bed covers off my bed and shook them. "Let's look under the mattress."

I knew it wasn't under there since the mattress sat on top of some storage that was built into the camper. But if it was going to make her happy, I was willing to take everything out of the camper so we could find it.

"I told you Mason stole them," she continued to say every time we'd move something or pull something up to look under it.

"I'm afraid I don't see them." I braced myself for the hissy fit she was about to throw as I watched her chest heave up and down from the breaths she took in and out of her nose.

"Maybe we can look again." It wouldn't hurt. "I just don't think he took them."

"Oh." She threw her hands up in the air. "Are you going to tell me it's the John Swift curse, and my pearls just vanished? Poof." She was getting snarky now. "All good." She brushed her hands off in front of her.

Her eyes narrowed. Her jaw tensed. Her fist clenched.

"I'm going to go into his camper and look. He can't stop me." She twirled on the balls of her hiking boots and left the camper.

"Lord, please help whoever took her pearls," I said, wondering if we should just all pack up and head on back to the Happy Trails Campground, where we were all happy.

By the time I made it out of the camper, Mary Elizabeth had gone over to Mason's camper with him on her heels. They were in an all-out cat fight.

"What are you going to do about this?" Abby questioned with a scared look on her face. "They don't care." She gestured to Agnes, Queenie, and Dirk.

All three of them were still crunching down on the nachos. I was jealous.

"What do you want me to do?" I snapped back at Abby. "The pearls are gone. I took everything apart in the camper. You and I both know she had them on. I did hear the banter between her and Mason where he tried to buy them off her. He even flirted with her."

"It doesn't make him a thief." Abby was quick to not have any conflict. It was just her quiet nature.

"No, but it does seem fishy since he's the one so interested in them." I didn't bother going to get between Mason and Mary Elizabeth because she'd take him and me down with one lash of her tongue. He would soon find it out.

Soon was real soon.

He staggered out of his camper from the top of the steps after Mary Elizabeth gave him a hard push backwards.

"She's your mom." He looked at me like I had three heads.

"Yeah. I know the consequences. Listen, if you took them, it's best to just give them back." I wondered if reasoning with him would work.

"If I took them? I didn't take them." He ran his hand through his hair when we all heard some slamming noises coming from the camper. "She's going to tear my stuff up."

"Just give them back." There was truly no other explanation.

"What's going on?" Ritchie had come over to the group.

"Mary Elizabeth's pearls are gone, and she thinks Mason took them, since he offered to buy them from her." Dirk scooped up a piece of steak with a nacho that dripped with cheese and stuffed it into his mouth.

"He was really wanting them, and if that's the case, maybe he should leave camp," Ritchie said. "I'm about to head home. Do you want me to call the police?"

"Yes. We do! Call the police! Call Hank Sharp!" Mary Elizabeth stood at the open door of the camper with her hands on her hips. "Tell them to bring the paddy wagon and take this thief away!"

"Yeah! Call the police!" Mason yelled at Mary Elizabeth when she marched down the steps and back to the group.

He and Mary Elizabeth stood nose to nose. Neither one backed down.

"It's the curse." Agnes's eyes glowed at the prospect of it.

"That's silly." What was silly was that I was the only one who didn't think it was the curse at this point.

"Go on and run all over the place to look for your precious pearls." Mason was being a jerk now.

"No wonder Sue Ann left you." Mary Elizabeth glared at him. "You are a no-good, dirty lying dog, and she deserves more in a man, if that's what you want to call yourself, than you."

"If you all think you're going to follow me and Dirk around tomorrow, because we are going to find the treasure, you can forget it." His finger circled the five of us. "You're on your own. You can go back to your little hillbilly campground for that matter and leave."

"You don't have to name call." Queenie stood up. "I think I've lost my appetite."

It was cute how Queenie threw away her empty plate. She'd not lost her appetite—she'd fed it. Still. She was trying to say she was picking Mary Elizabeth's side.

"We don't need you anyways." Mary Elizabeth walked over to Agnes and tried to take her plate. Agnes had a death grip on it but let go when Mary Elizabeth gave her a look of death. "We've got our own maps of real treasure hunters. Ain't that right, Agnes?"

"Yeah. That's right. My Graham, he was a treasure hunter," she said proudly.

"Yes'm, you told us." Dirk had finally found his voice. "Why don't we all go to our campers and get a good night's sleep."

"I'm waiting up for the police." Mary Elizabeth sat down in a chair in front of the campfire. "Ritchie left, so it won't be long." She crossed her arms and wasn't about to budge.

"Fine. You do what you think you need to do, but we are going to bed." Mason tugged on Dirk's shirt, and they both left.

"I'm not going to sit out here and get eaten up by chiggers." Queenie swatted at her ankle before she skipped back to the camper, soon followed by Agnes and Abby.

In the distance, the sky lit up as heat lightning rippled through the darkness.

"Are you sure?" I asked Mary Elizabeth. "It looks like rain might be moving in."

"I'm more sure than ever that I'm not going to leave this chair. They might try to get out of here with my pearls when we are sleeping. That's their treasure." Mary Elizabeth looked hurt. "I just can't believe this. My mama would be so upset."

"I'm not sure where they are, but once Ritchie gets the police here, they will help look and get to the bottom of it." I rubbed her on the shoulder. "Are you sure you won't just come in and watch from the kitchen table? It really does look like it's going to rain."

"Not in a million years. Hell or high water, it's what I'm doing." She dug her feet deeper into the grass. I left her to do exactly what she wanted.

No one in this world was going to tell Mary Elizabeth Moberly what to do. That included me.

EIGHT

"She's gone and lost her ever-loving mind." Agnes had the curtain pulled back, looking out into the dark, rainy night. "Mary Elizabeth is going to catch a cold, get pneumonia, and die."

The campfire had long gone extinguished from the storm coming through. I'd gone back out and given her an umbrella, but she refused it. Mary Elizabeth was making a point, and she wasn't going to budge. It would take a bulldozer to pick her up and move her until Mason gave her back the strand of pearls she'd accused him of stealing.

"Lightning is going to hit her." Abby leaned over Agnes's shoulder, biting her lip. "I think you need to get her seen by the doctor, because no one in their right mind would risk their life for a set of pearls."

"You don't know Mary Elizabeth. Once her mind is on something, you can't get it off of it." I failed to tell how Mary Elizabeth had sat outside of the county fair offices for three days to turn in the beauty pageant form for me to enter. It wasn't like anyone was dying to win the title, and no other mother sat out there for three days. I didn't even want to be in the darn thing, but Mary Elizabeth Moberly had it in her head that her adoptive daughter would be the debutante.

She'd had it in her mind that I'd had a hard life, and no matter what, we were going to show people how we pulled ourselves up by our bootstraps and made it in life. I was perfectly fine with my life, since I knew I was going to get out of there on my eighteenth birthday.

"I've been looking out at the entrance." Queenie had been sitting in the driver's captain chair looking out the window. She swiveled the chair around. "I still don't see no headlights from the police."

"I'm sure Ritchie told them the story, and it wasn't on the priority list." I looked out the window at Mary Elizabeth. She'd not moved an iota. She had her hands placed on her knees, and she stared at Mason's camper.

Mason and Dirk didn't seem to care. The lights were out in their RVs, and the pounding rain didn't bother them any.

"We can't just sit up all night and watch her make a fool of herself." Agnes switched places with Abby. "I'm going to get some shuteye, so y'all go on and get out of my bedroom."

"I'm not going to let you sleep out here." I'd planned for her and Mary Elizabeth to sleep in my bed since they were the oldest, and the mattress was made specifically for my camper. "Queenie, you go with her and Abby, and I'll watch Mary Elizabeth."

"I don't know why we are watching her." Abby pulled the curtain shut. "If that clap of thunder didn't light a torch under her hiney, I don't think nothing will."

Queenie and Agnes went to the back and got ready for bed. Abby made the coffee so we only had to flip on the switch in the morning, which was just a few hours away, while I made the couches into a makeshift bed for me and her.

Abby and I didn't say much. Both of us felt deeply disturbed at how Mary Elizabeth had acted.

"We looked everywhere for those pearls." Abby's voice pierced the dark as both of us lay there.

The rain continued to knock on the roof of the camper. I couldn't help but think Mary Elizabeth was shivering out there. Once one of these dog-days-of-summer rains got into your bones, it was hard to shake it off.

"Where do you think it is? Do you think Mason took them?" Abby rolled over to her side to face me from the little couch. Abby and I had done some investigating on our own before and with great results, I add.

"I don't know. I mean, he did make such a big deal about them when he noticed them." I recalled how hungry his eyes looked when he saw the pearls around Mary Elizabeth's neck. "He continued to offer her more and more money for them, but she refused. They've been in her family for so long and they're so much a part of her identity that I'm not sure what she'll do if we don't find them."

"What are we going to do?" she asked.

"I don't think Ritchie went to the police, because I think Hank would've been told, and he'd have been here." I remembered the CB radio Dottie had given me. "If they aren't here in the morning"—I glanced at the digital clock I had on the wall and realized morning was just a couple hours away—"then I'm going to hook up the CB Dottie gave me just to tell her to tell Hank about the missing pearls."

"You have a CB?" Abby popped up, leaning on her elbow. "You should've called before the storm because the rain will hurt the waves."

"I don't know anything about the darn thing, but you can try your hand at it." I was going to get up and let her work with it, but she stopped me.

"It won't do us any good now. The thunder and lightning won't help. Might's well wait until the morning." She rolled back the other way, and before I knew it, the sound of snoring filled the camper.

I got up and looked one more time at Mary Elizabeth. She was still sitting there staring at Mason's camper.

I shook my head and lay back down on the couch, tugging the blankets up to my chin.

As I recalled the conversation from start to finish, the rhythm of the rain sounded like a song and put me right to sleep like a lullaby.

NINE

"Get up!" Agnes shook me by my shoulder. "Mason and Dirk are going at it. Mary Elizabeth is encouraging Dirk."

"What?" I bolted up from being sound asleep, throwing the cover off me.

Agnes already had the door open with Queenie following behind her. I grabbed my hiking boots and put them on without lacing them up.

"Sock him!" Mary Elizabeth looked like a drowned rat as she hooked her arms like she was in the boxing ring. "Sock him good too!"

Dirk and Mason danced around on their toes in a circle with their fists up.

"What is going on here?" I stomped through the mud puddles to reach them and put my arms out. "Has everyone lost their minds?" I looked between them.

"Get out of the way. Dirk is gonna give that thief exactly what he's got coming." Mary Elizabeth punched the air a few times.

"You've gotten really good at your form," Queenie encouraged Mary Elizabeth. The wrong thing to do. The grass was soaked. "Strike class has really been helping you."

Mary Elizabeth and Queenie started to talk about the Jazzercise class, while I tried to stop the real fight.

"Leave us alone, Mae," Dirk warned me, never looking away from Mason. "He's got this coming to him. Your mom is right. He's a thief."

"Not a thief. The silver is anyone's to look for. Ask Queenie. She knows. She's the historian here." Mason tightened his fists and moved them up to his face.

"We agreed when Sue Ann left that I'd get her share. Not just the twenty-five percent. Half. Half of whatever we find out there, and now you are saying I'm not getting what is owed to me." Dirk jabbed the air a couple of times, and Mason pulled back, barely missing getting punched in the face.

"Stop this right now!" I screamed. "This is ridiculous."

"Get him!" Mary Elizabeth screamed.

"Stop it now! You are grown men, and you are my mother," I said through gritted teeth. I bounced between them, ignoring the mud flinging up from under my feet.

"Did you just call me your mother?" Mary Elizabeth got a little too excited and flung her arms around my neck, practically squeezing the life out of me. "Thank you," she gushed and kissed me before she let go. She turned to Mason. "Keep the pearls, loser." Her nose curled. "They are worth a lot, but hearing Mae call me her mother is worth the loss. If I had to get those pearls stolen to hear this"—she looked at me, tears in her eyes—"it's worth it. Hearing that is worth more than those pearls."

"Is that really all it took?" Agnes snarled.

"That doesn't settle this." Dirk pointed to Mason. "I'm going to get half of whatever we find today and tomorrow." He took a step forward and jabbed Mason in the chest with his finger. "Got it?"

"Yeah. We'll see." Mason's jaw set. He didn't bother watching Dirk stomp back to his camper. "Ahem," he cleared his throat. "I'm going to tell you one more time, and then we aren't going to revisit this again." He jabbed a finger toward Mary Elizabeth. "I didn't take your stupid pearls. Now, be ready in ten minutes to head out."

"We aren't going with you." I stepped up and glared at him. Forget that I was sinking into the wet ground. "You're a jerk. If anyone took the pearls, we know it's you, and when the police get here, we will make sure to tell them everything."

"The police aren't coming at least until tomorrow. No one is coming or going." Mason laughed. "The roads have washed out from the storm."

"What?" My entire insides deflated. "We can't leave even if we wanted to?"

I was going to suggest to my group that we just leave and not worry about the treasure.

"Nope. Ritchie came back last night and knocked on my door when he saw Mary Elizabeth sprawled out in the chair, asleep." Mason eyed Mary Elizabeth.

"I was doing no such thing. I saw him." Mary Elizabeth twitched, a sure sign of her lying.

"Regardless, what exactly did he say?" I asked and turned around to look at Ritchie's little cabin in the middle of the field.

"What does it matter?" Mason acted as if I was putting him out. "The roads are closed. I'm sure it'll all dry out by the time we all leave tomorrow." He turned and headed toward his camper. "Five minutes, ladies, or I'm leaving without you."

"'Five minutes, ladies,'" Queenie mocked Mason with a curled lip and squished-up nose. "I'll give him five minutes." She turned to Mary Elizabeth. "Come on. We need to get you in the camper for a hot shower and a cup of coffee."

While they all took Mary Elizabeth into the camper, I decided to head over to see Ritchie to learn exactly what he knew about the roads and if he went to the police station like Agnes had suggested.

There wasn't any electricity running to his cabin, and I couldn't tell if he was asleep or up. I took my chances and knocked on the door anyway. When he greeted me in a pair of underwear and nothing else, I got my answer.

"Oh. Crap." He was decent enough to use his hands to cover himself. "I thought you were a guy. Let me put some pants on." He shut the door on me.

I could hear some rustling in the cabin. Probably where there was no light and he couldn't see, since I'd apparently awakened him from a dead sleep.

"Sorry 'bout that." He yawned and stretched his hands over his head. "I got in late, and that rain makes me sleep like a wee little baby."

He stepped out of the cabin, and his bare feet sank into the wet grass, mud squishing up between his toes.

"What can I do you for?" He crossed his arms in front of him.

"We still haven't found the pearls. It's my understanding the roads have been washed out, and no one is coming in or out of here." I ignored the sounds of Mason and Dirk behind me. Ritchie didn't, though. He was watching every move they made from over my shoulder. "Did you go to the police station about the missing pearls?"

"I was headed there when the big storm came, and I knew I didn't have no time to go there and be back here before the gravel washed away. So I made me an executive decision. The safety of the campers during a wash-out is more important than a pair of pearls to me. Safety first. That's what they teach you in Scouts." He sucked in a deep breath; his eyes bored into me like he was prepared to challenge me if I dared say something.

"So you didn't go to the police station? I just want to be clear." My shoulders dropped when I realized he was barely listening to me. I snapped my fingers in front of his face.

"No." He shook his head. "I didn't. But I'll try to get out today while you're hunting."

It was the best I was going to get from him, and I knew it.

"Fine. Just let me know." I turned around when I didn't even get an acknowledging grunt, much less any words from him.

Mason and Dirk must've made up because on my way back to my camper, I watched the two of them disappear into the woods where the mouth of the trail led to what they believed was the John Swift silver mine.

The sun was trying to peek out over top of the mountainous area. If it would just pop out, it might help dry up some of the road, though I knew that road was literally covered from the bridge of trees on the way here and the sun would have to penetrate through them to even start to warm the gravel and dirt.

The mud squished underneath my boots, and I took them off once I stepped up on the step before entering the camper.

"Anything?" Agnes greeted me with a cup of steaming coffee after I shut the camper door.

"No." I shook my head and took the coffee mug. "Ritchie said he had to make an executive decision about the safety of the campers or the pearls. He thinks he's in charge of us and wanted to be here in case something went wrong."

The first sip of the coffee instantly made me feel somewhat better. They'd already cleaned up the covers from the couches. I sat down in one of the café chairs and curled my hands around the mug, bringing it up to my mouth to enjoy the warm liquid.

"What are we going to do?" Queenie asked and looked around at all five of us. She was spraying the bug spray all over her body, including her clothes.

After Queenie doused herself in the stuff, she handed it off to Abby, who handed it off to Agnes, who handed it off to Mary Elizabeth.

"We are going to go find that treasure." Mary Elizabeth ran her hand across her neck where her pearls used to hang. "If I don't have my treasure, Mason won't have his. That means we have to find the John Swift silver before he does."

"That's music to my ears." Agnes gave a vicious grin. "I've got the food backpack." She flung the bigger bag on her back.

"Here, spray yourself good." Mary Elizabeth held the spray out to me. "When you were a kid, you fought me tooth and nail for me to spray you."

These women were out for blood. Even the poor bugs had no chance with them. They say you never cross a Southern woman, and here Mason had crossed two. The John Swift curse had nothing on a scorned Southern woman.

Mary Elizabeth decided to spray me herself, even my clothes. I batted her away before she got near my arms and face.

With everyone all bug-sprayed up, we were out the door in no time.

"How on earth did you sleep in that rain?" I asked Mary Elizabeth as I locked the door to the camper, since I was the last one out.

"Honey, I'm tougher than you know." She winked, and we headed into the woods.

"Let's go find that treasure." I smiled.

"I got my treasure this morning." She patted me on the back as she referred to me calling her Mom.

TEN

"Who does he think he is?" Even though Mary Elizabeth had said she was letting it go until we could get some police in here, she didn't. "He can't tell Sue Ann she can't be here when he's here. He isn't Father Nature, God, or the owner of the Daniel Boone National Forest." She swung the walking stick at all the low-lying branches to smack them out of the way.

At least she was getting some energy out and would probably sleep like a baby tonight. Or maybe a big nap this afternoon if we took a break. She claimed she was up all night, but according to Ritchie, when he came back to the campsite, she was snoring to beat the band.

"Let's focus on the treasure." Agnes glanced back. She was leading the group and had Graham's map in one hand and the compass in the other. "According to the map, the Furnace is this way."

"How far?" Queenie pushed the glittery headband up on her forehead a little more.

"Three miles." It rolled off Agnes's tongue like it was just a jaunt around the bend.

"Dear Lord!" Mary Elizabeth huffed. "Three miles? Why didn't we camp closer?"

"There's no camping in the forest. Only the designated areas." Abby was so sweet and really took the time to explain to Mary Elizabeth how John Swift couldn't just put his treasure where anyone could just find it.

Every few thousand feet, we'd stop for a drink of water and maybe a little taste of chocolate to keep us going. Abby and I continued to take turns hiking with the food backpack. There were a few grunts and grumbles from the group, especially when we had to climb over a little more brush than the typical fallen logs or rocks. The farther we hiked into the forest, the thicker the vines, grassy areas, and rocky areas, making it a little more challenging. I kept an eye on Agnes and Mary Elizabeth, not that Queenie was much younger, but she was in better physical shape with her Jazzercise.

"Do you hear that?" Agnes perked up and turned her ear.

We all stopped. The sounds of birds chirping and a faint bubbling sound filled the silence.

"I think that's the small branch in the journal." Agnes handed the papers to Abby. "Read that."

"To go to the Furnace to the ore, climb the rock to the left hand, steer a due south course till you come to a small branch. You will find the way very rough. Then go to the branch to the head without crossing. Then due east to the top of the ridge out of the cliff country."

"That's enough for now." Agnes took the papers back from Abby. "After we get due east past the branch, we will revisit the journal. I think we are close. I remember my Graham talking about it."

"You lead the way." I was started to get excited, even though Hank had told me it was really a tall tale. Just the fun of being with the group was enough for me. Making good memories was also very important.

"Climb the rock to the left." Agnes repeated over and over as the sound of a creek got closer and closer.

All of our eyes were focused up, and we looked around to help find this rock to the left. There were a lot of cliffs and rocks but nothing due south per John Swift's instructions.

"That's that?" Abby pointed to a mossy-looking structure. "I think it's the rock. It'll take us to another level of the forest."

"Should we climb it?" Mary Elizabeth climbed over a downed log and took a high step up on one of many ledges that we could carefully climb to the top.

"I think we should." I encouraged everyone to make a move because we'd never know unless we did it.

"I think so too." Agnes's eyes grew big. She held the map and pointed to a spot. "We passed the three beeches, and if we climb the rock, we can go east." There was an X on Graham's map. "Abby, let me see Swift's map."

Abby took off the food backpack and opened the front zippered pocket, where she'd put the maps in a Ziploc bag in case something happened and it got wet.

"If you lay Graham's map overtop of Swift's…" Agnes put the maps on top of each other. The X Graham had put on his map and the mine Swift had named West Mine practically lined up together. "This has to be the one Graham had been looking for."

Agnes's face glowed. Some pride and some joy all tied together.

Without even asking what we thought, she handed Abby back the map and took off up the mossy rock. Abby put the map back in the Ziploc and zippered pocket of the pack, replacing the backpack on her back.

"Be careful," I told Mary Elizabeth, who I made climb in front of me just in case she fell and took me down with her, allowing me to soften her fall.

There was a small cliff that led up to the next one, like stepping stones to the top. The moss was slick from all the rain we'd had, which made it slippery to climb fast, so we all took a step and even told each other, "Be careful on that one. It's really slippery."

Once we all got to the top of the rock, we sat down on the rock and took a small water break to catch our breaths. Climbing the rock was a lot harder than I thought it was going to be. I was using muscles I'd not used in a long time or maybe ever. I already longed to go to bed, but we were still just a couple of hours into the hike.

Some shuffling sounds caused all of us to look over our shoulders. We listened for a long pause before we turned to look at each other. Silently, our eyes shifted to each other, as if we were trying to figure out what each one was thinking.

"What is that?" I asked.

Agnes pushed herself up and held up a finger for us to stay while she crept over toward the shuffling sound. I'm not sure why, but we all felt like Agnes knew what she was doing, and she was the Mason of our group.

"Is it a bear?" Mary Elizabeth looked at me with big eyes. "Just like John Swift said in the journal."

"What did he say again?" Queenie dug into her backpack and pulled out the set of papers she'd taken from the Historical Society.

"It's probably just another group of treasure hunters." Abby made the most sense, and I elected to believe her.

"I'm sure Abby is right." I was happy and relieved to see Agnes come back.

"I didn't see anything." Agnes didn't look at us. "Let's go." She grabbed her backpack and put it on. By accident, her eyes met mine. Something in them said she wasn't really telling the full truth, but I couldn't put my finger on it. "We are almost there."

"You take the end of the line," I told Abby so I could be behind Agnes and try to figure out what she was hiding.

Agnes stood at the front of our little line.

"Me, Mae, Queenie, Mary Elizabeth, and Abby." She pointed to each of us when she said our name. "We are all here. Are we all good?"

As soon as we all nodded, Agnes started us on the last leg of the journey to the West Mine.

"Our first clue to check off is the creek, right?" I asked Agnes, fully knowing it was where we were headed, but I wanted to open the lines of communication with her.

"Yes." The one-word answer and her pinched lips were sure signs Agnes Swift was hiding something. Then something just hit me. "Agnes Swift. Swift. Graham Swift. John Swift."

"It took you this long to figure out Graham was believed to be a descendant of *the* John Swift?" Agnes's lips relaxed, as did her face. "Why do you think it was so important for Graham to find it?"

"Gosh. I never even thought. So is this why Hank thinks the legend is just a tall tale?" I asked her, hoping to open her up even more.

"Graham's family had so many generations that were so proud of the legend, and Graham was too. We spent so many nights alone, me and my daughter." She was referring to Hank's mom. We'd come to a nice embankment next to a small brook. The foliage was growing close to the ground, so we all walked next to the babbling water, thanks to the heavy rain.

Agnes continued, "I think that's why they decided to follow Ellis around the world for her modeling career, leaving Hank here."

There was a small family rift between Agnes and Hank's mother. Hank was in the middle, but he was more on the side of his granny Agnes than his own mom. It was a long story that I'd been able to piece together little by little as I'd gotten closer to Hank. This was a new discovery.

"Hank and I talked a lot about the legend, and he came to the conclusion it was all false after he'd spent a few years in his teens out here looking." She smiled. "You and I both know Hank has a lot of pride and doesn't like to be wrong. So I think that's why he is adamant about it being a tall tale."

It made a lot of sense now that I thought about Hank and how he was very private about his younger years. Hank was probably the last type of guy I thought I'd see myself with. He was a little rough around the edges. He liked being outside. He was not the southern gentleman that I liked. Nor had he even lived the lifestyle I'd gotten accustomed to with Paul West. I think it was probably his rougher side that appealed to me because underneath a few of those layers, he'd do anything to keep me safe and happy.

"I think we are here," Agnes gasped. She pointed to the opening of the stream into a much larger pond. One of the many gems the Daniel Boone National Park had to offer.

"That trickling sound is making my water drop." Mary Elizabeth did a little tinkle dance. Her head swiveled around as if she were looking for a spot to do her business.

Agnes's jaw dropped, making her mouth part before a big wide smile drew up on her face. "Up there."

"You want me to go up there to go potty?" Mary Elizabeth shrugged, while Agnes didn't pay a bit of attention to her. Agnes was pointing to the rock. I didn't stop Mary Elizabeth when she started to make her way around the hanging rock and climb up.

"Oh! It's the rock." Abby pulled the pack off her back and got the journal back out. She began to read, "'At the branch head without crossing, then due east to the top of the ridge out of the clift country, then along the ridge to the right-hand side, and there will appear a place that is higher than the other. The hanging rock.'" Abby drew her eyes up from the paper and looked at the formation that appeared to hang over us from where we were standing.

"The rock!" Queenie bounced on her toes and clapped her hands. "We've got to go up there."

"Let Mary Elizabeth tell us what's up there when she gets back." I covered my eyes from the sun. A couple of rocks tumbled down. "Mary Elizabeth? You okay?" I hollered up but didn't get a response.

The four of us stood there looking up as a few more pebbles fell.

"Do you think she's okay?" Abby gave me a worried look.

"We need to go up there according to the map, so let's just meet her up there." Queenie made a good point.

"Watch out!" Agnes yelled when a few larger rocks rolled down and fell into the water below.

The heat beat down over the rock, and when I looked at it, something shadowed the sun, as if there were a small eclipse.

"Avalanche!" I screamed and ran to the side, covering my head with my arms before I knocked Agnes out of the way with my body.

I heard a loud splash into the water—then silence.

I gulped and looked up. Mary Elizabeth stood on the hanging rock above the branch and waved.

"All done!" She grinned, having no idea what just happened to us down here.

"Is everyone okay?" I asked and made sure to look at them. They all looked okay. "Did you know big rocks fell like that?" I asked them since this was my first time here.

"It wasn't a rock," Abby said, her voice cracking.

We all looked over to where she pointed.

"My pearls!" Mary Elizabeth screamed from above.

Mason Cavanaugh lay face up, eyes open, floating in the water, with Mary Elizabeth's pearls in the grip of his hand.

"The curse." Agnes's words sent chills along my spine.

ELEVEN

Mary Elizabeth let out a scream that would wake the dead… well, it didn't wake Mason Cavanaugh.

"My pearls!" Mary Elizabeth continued to yell as she fought the terrain to come back down to where we were. She ran to the edge of the water, and before I could gather my wits about me, she did a belly flop, creating a big splash.

"Stop!" I was shocked Mary Elizabeth would jump in with a dead body, much less grab her pearls out of his dead hand. "That's evidence."

"Yeah! Evidence he stole them like I said." Her face flushed white, and her eyes grew big like she just realized what she'd just done. She turned back around, and the motion of the waves she'd created had Mason's body floating right toward her. "Get me out of here!" She started to fight the water as she tried to run toward us, leaving the pearls in his grip.

I stood at the edge, leaning over with my arm extended so she could grab it. The more motion she created in the water, the faster Mason's body caught up to her.

"Help me," she cried out and grasped my hand. I tugged. Her belly dragged along the edge and across the grass as I walked backwards, pulling her to safety.

"Grab him!" Agnes barked at me when I let go of Mary Elizabeth.

My adrenaline kicked in, and I did exactly what she said. I stepped into the water and grabbed Mason's arm before the tide shifted and dragged him up to the shore.

We all stood there for a second, looking at Mason as we tried to wrap our heads around what we were seeing. The sound of footsteps were as loud as thunder as they came toward us.

"I heard a scream." Sue Ann Jaffarian stood behind us. "What happened?" she asked and walked in between me and Mary Elizabeth. "Mason?" She screamed and fell to the ground. "Did you do CPR?" She didn't even wait for us to answer. She started to do mouth to mouth on him. "Idiots." She turned her head to me. "Help me."

"Okay." I wasn't really sure what to do since I seemed to be stuck in my head, and nothing was computing.

"Get out of the way." Sue Ann shoved me and started to do the chest compressions between the mouth-to-mouth resuscitation.

A couple of times Mary Elizabeth actually reached over as if she were going to get those darn pearls. I gave her the stink eye a couple of times, making her pull her hand back.

She did this for about five minutes until she had a complete breakdown. A flood of tears followed with sobs escaping her as she leaned her body over his, and primal sounds came out of her.

"I'm so sorry." I bent down and put an arm around her for comfort.

"No, you're not," she spat and jerked away, finding her footing to stand. "You!" She pointed to Mary Elizabeth. "You killed him. I saw you come down from there. You pushed him because you wanted those stupid pearls."

"How did you know about the pearls?" Agnes asked.

"Dirk told me when I saw him about an hour ago." She looked around. "Where is Dirk?"

"We've not seen him." I tried to be as calm as I could, since she'd just accused Mary Elizabeth of killing Mason.

"Now what?" Abby's voice cracked. "We don't have cell service. We can't get out of the campsite to get help."

"We have to carry him back. We can't leave him here." Sue Ann started to sob all over again. "I love you so much." She fell back to the ground.

It took a second, but I got everyone's attention, besides Sue Ann, and nodded for them to meet me out of earshot of her. Quietly, we all walked away.

"What are we going to do?" I directed my question at Agnes.

"Why are you looking at me?" she asked.

"Because you work around this stuff all day," I pointed out. "What do the police do when they get called to a murder scene?"

"We don't know it's murder, and you should ask yourself that same question," Queenie suggested with a little sarcasm.

"Just because I've found a couple of dead bodies…" I started to say before I was rudely interrupted.

"A couple?" Abby asked.

"Listen, I get that we are all tense here, but we are here, and we need to do something. Sue Ann is right about one thing."

"I didn't kill him." Mary Elizabeth jerked back. "I never saw him up there."

Her statement stuck in my head. She was on the same rock formation. How did she not see him.

"Not right about that." I sucked in a deep breath, curled my lips together, and let it out my nose while I looked at them underneath my brows. "She's right that we can't leave him here."

"I'm not carrying him." Queenie crossed her arms.

"Stop it." I shot her an eye. "We all have to carry some sort of part of him. You." I pointed to Abby. "You take a foot, while I take a wrist. Mary Elizabeth, you take a foot, and Queenie, you take a wrist with me."

"What about them two?" Queenie flung her hand at Agnes then at Sue Ann.

"They are going to get us out of here. They know the way." I licked my lips and thought back to the crime scenes I'd had the unfortunate time being involved in. "Hank would mark off the scene, take photos, and then look for evidence."

"He fell from the rock. I bet he saw us and leaned over too far." Abby made a good case, but by the look on

Agnes's face, I could tell she was thinking something completely different.

"What is it, Agnes?" I asked.

"I don't know. I wouldn't count him out being murdered." She glanced around. "You go up to the top of the rock and see if he left his backpack up there or where his maps are. When he left this morning, he had his gear. Where is it?"

"I've got my phone so I can take photos." Abby pulled her phone from her pocket.

"Mary Elizabeth and I can gather some rocks and make a circumference around what we think is the crime scene down here." Queenie also made a good suggestion.

"This is great teamwork." I smiled and nodded, happy to see that we were all starting to come to our senses, but it wasn't far from my mind that there were two people here that had some threatening words with Mason, even if one of them was my adoptive mother. And she just so happened to have been up on that rock when Mason had fallen to his death.

"Sue Ann." I put a hand on her back. This time she didn't jerk away from my touch. "Agnes Swift works at the Normal police station, and we are going to treat this like a crime scene and do the things the police would do if they were here."

"Did she confess?" Sue Ann referred to Mary Elizabeth.

"No. I'm sure she didn't push him off the rock." I had the need to defend my adoptive mom even if I wasn't sure what happened. I did know that she'd never, ever murder someone. "But I'm going to go up to the rock and look for his equipment while Agnes checks out some things around here."

Sue Ann quickly nodded in agreement.

"Please don't touch his body until Agnes looks at him and we carry him out." I knew that would be met with a gush of tears.

"I still loved him." She brushed her hand across her cheek. "We were together for a long time."

"I know." I pinched my lips together and left her alone. The others were off doing exactly what they'd planned to do, and now it was my turn to climb the rock.

With each step, I tried to see through the eyes of Mary Elizabeth. What I thought was beautiful was a sight for sore eyes in her mind, so it was difficult to see through the beauty of nature. The climb was steep but not so much so that Mary Elizabeth would have a hard time climbing to the top to go tinkle.

Once at the top, I looked both ways. The sun was bright and almost blinding. Had Mason accidentally walked off the rock, not seeing the edge in the glare of the sunlight? He wasn't wearing sunglasses, and I wasn't either. I had to shield my eyes to get a good look.

To the right was where it appeared in a lower area. Carefully, I walked to the edge of the rock, noticing there wasn't a slick spot or a wet spot from the rain. This knocked out my theory that he'd slipped and fallen. The rock was dry as a bone. The water was crystal clear, as far as the eye could see. The view was spectacular, and I wondered if this was the last thing Mason had seen.

"Abby!" I yelled down when I peeked over the side. My stomach felt like I was on a big roller coaster and the first huge hill was approaching. The anticipation of the thought of Mason falling off here curled in my stomach. It was a long way down. The impact of hitting the water must've been what actually stopped his heart after he'd either fallen or someone killed him.

There weren't any uneven spots or gravel where I stood.

"What?" I heard Abby holler back without me looking down. I just couldn't look down.

"Am I standing about the spot where Mason landed in the water?" I asked because I wanted to make sure there was nothing there for him to have slipped on.

"Yes!" she answered.

"Can you also read to me the journal entry where we left off? And yell it out." I took a big step back and away from the edge, making me breathe a little easier.

"'Along the ridge out of the clift.'"

I knew the clift she was referring to was the overhanging rock I was standing on.

"'There will appear a place that is higher than the other.'"

I looked around as she read Swift's journal.

"'Go in a low gap. Leave the high knob to the right.'"

"To the right." I glanced around that way and saw a low spot.

"'Go down, and you will see a hanging rock and a rock that seems to have fallen from the other. Go in betwixt them, and you are very near the spot. You will find the opening of the mine.'"

"That's all for now!" Our voices echoed back as we'd been speaking. "Go to the low spot." I told myself the high points I'd gotten out of the text Abby had said to make sure I got the main markers Swift had stated. "Hanging rock and another rock."

I walked down into the low spot and looked for any sign of Mason's gear. It had to be here somewhere. I shifted my gaze up and saw the exact rock from Swift's journal. The rock was just a few yards away, but the brush was so thick, it took more time than I had anticipated.

The chiggers were biting every naked piece of skin on me they could find. I'd smack the spot where I felt them gnaw into me, but it was already too late. The nasty bugs had already gotten me, and little bumps showed it.

"I should've put that bug spray on my arms." I regretted not listening to Mary Elizabeth now. I smacked away a few more of the critters on my way down the gap, heading to the hanging rock, as John Swift put it. "A cave," I gasped when I got to the underhang. "Is this where you met the bear?" I asked out loud as if someone was going to answer me.

"It might be." The voice caused me to jump around.

"Dirk." I put my hand up to my chest. "You scared me."

"Sorry about that." He grinned and looked around. "Where's your friends?"

"They are with…" I stopped when I realized he didn't know about Mason. "Dirk, Mason is…" I gulped and watched his eyes search my face.

"He's in the cave looking for the treasure." He laughed and pointed inside the opening. "What's wrong?" The smile fell.

"Mason isn't in the cave. He… um… fell off the cliff and into the water. And, um…" I blinked a few times to get it together. "He is dead, and my friends are with his body."

"Dead?" He cried out. "No. You're mistaken." He ran his hand through his hair before he darted into the cave. "Mason! Hey, man, where are you? Yell back if you can hear me!"

"Dirk," I called after him and looked into the dark abyss. "Dirk!"

There was no way I was going in there without some sort of light, and I knew I didn't have a flashlight on me.

"Mason!" The echo of Dirk's voice bounced off the walls of the cave. Chills traveled up my body at the sound of his desperate cry. "Come on, man, answer me!"

"Dirk!" I'd put my hands up around my mouth as a megaphone. "Dirk! Please come back and see for yourself."

The silence was deafening. The darkness was frightening. I took a step out of the cave and looked up at the sunshine trickling through the leaves. I jerked my head toward the cave when I heard heavy footsteps approaching the mouth.

"No." Dirk shook his head, his jaw clenched. "Can't be." His nostrils flared as his chest heaved up and down. "No way. He was so careful. No way."

"Please just come with me. We need to get him out of the forest." I pushed my hands in the pockets of my pants and waited for what I was telling him to process in his jumbled head. "We need to go before we lose sunlight."

"Our stuff." He walked over to a brushy area, where he uncovered their backpacks and a couple of other sacks. "I can't leave it here."

"I can help." I walked over and let him decide what he needed me to carry, and soon we were on our way. "Did you know he left the cave?" I asked.

"No." Dirk was walking behind me, following me to the others and Mason. "He was sure this was the cave. We'd been to this location so many times because it was one of the first places John Swift talked about in his journal. Really it's a rookie move."

I turned around when he didn't continue. His eyes were hollow, and his face was flushed.

"Let's stop for a second. Do you have any water in these?" I asked since I hadn't planned on being gone for so long, so I didn't bring any water with me.

"Yeah." He blinked a few times and pointed to one of the bags he'd given me.

Without asking him any more questions, I decided to just unzip some of the openings of the bag until I found a bottle and handed it to him.

Five minutes went by until he finally screwed the lid back on the bottle and looked up at me.

"We've been here hundreds of times over the past five years. He's always been so careful. This just doesn't make sense." He held the bottle out to me. "Do you want a drink?"

"No." I shook my head. "I'm good. You need to drink it."

He did. He finished it off and stuck it in his backpack.

"You said he was on a cliff?" Dirk asked with disbelief in his tone.

"It was the rock that overlooks the mouth of the stream." I didn't recall John Swift's actual wording from the journal. "It was in the journal."

"Yeah. I know the rock. But there was no reason for him to go there." Dirk stood back up, signaling it was time for us to continue on our way. "He was exploring the cave like we'd done so many times before."

"Where were you?" I asked.

"I, um…" There was an uncomfortable pause. "I…"

I turned around, suspicious of his behavior. His face was flushed, and sweat dripped down his face.

"Are you okay?" I asked, stopping us.

"Fine." He ran the sleeve of his shirt across his face. "I think I just need to get back to camp."

"Do you think you can help us with Mason?" I asked. "It's just a few more feet that way."

"Of course." He took a few steps, making me proceed.

I figured it best not to say anything else so he could preserve his energy for our hike back to the campsite. The last thing the Laundry Club gals and I needed was another body to try to carry.

"There you are," Mary Elizabeth greeted me after Dirk and I had climbed down the rock to the opening of the lake. "We were starting to worry." Her eyes shifted to Dirk. "He doesn't look so good."

Dirk shoved past me and right over to Mason's body. He stood there with a look of shock on his face. Sue Ann was still hovering over the corpse.

Agnes, Queenie, and Abby walked over to me and Mary Elizabeth.

"I think he's in shock. We need to hurry back," I told the group. "Did you find anything?" I asked Agnes.

"No. You?" We started to walk over to Dirk and Sue Ann.

"There's some unanswered questions I have, but Dirk is in no shape to answer them." I shrugged.

"We need to get back." Agnes started to bark some orders.

"Who do you think you are? You can't just tell us what to do. He was our friend." Dirk's tone was stiff.

"I'm Agnes Swift, an employee of the Normal Police Station, and I hereby deputize myself to look into the murder until the law can drive into camp." All of her little, elderly body stood firm.

"Murder?" Dirk's eyes popped open. "You think he was murdered?"

"I'm not sure, but we are treating it as such since the three of you"—she pointed to him, Sue Ann, and Mary Elizabeth—"did threaten that you'd like him dead."

"Now wait a minute." Sue Ann stood up. "You've lost your marbles."

"Yep. The heat has fried your brain," Mary Elizabeth chirped.

"Stop it!" Dirk screamed. "This is ridiculous. We need to get him back to camp before the sun starts to set and the trees cover the forest with darkness. Then we'll be stuck out here."

TWELVE

"What the hell?" Ritchie ran over to the tree line from the campfire when he noticed us walking out, carrying Mason's body.

"In the tent," I grunted from packing my share of the weight. "Let's put him in there."

"In this heat?" Sue Ann cried out from behind us.

"You want to put him in your camper? Then you can carry him to wherever it is you're staying." Mary Elizabeth had about enough. After Agnes took the pearls for evidence back at the water, Mary Elizabeth had been spitting nails under her breath ever since.

"Fine." Sue Ann shook her head and nuzzled against Dirk's chest.

"Wait a minute." Ritchie was in a panic. He jumped around each of us as we walked to the tent. "What the hell happened?"

"Ritchie"—Agnes jerked around—"you say another curse word, and I'm gonna tell your grandmother. We attend the same Sunday school lesson." She shook a finger at him. "Do you understand me?"

"Yes'm, but I'm just trying to figure out what happened here. I ain't never had no one die and certainly never expected someone as trained as Mason Cavanaugh to have the curse laid upon him." Ritchie continued to follow alongside of us, his eyes on Mason.

"It was no curse. Someone wants you to think it's the curse." Agnes made a lot of sense, and I wondered if she was right.

"Agnes, what if that's it?" I couldn't believe I'd not thought of that.

"We will talk about this once we get him in there," she whispered. "Not around those three." She nodded at Dirk, Ritchie, and Sue Ann, who were huddled around Mason's body.

"What are you doing with them?" Dirk asked Sue Ann. "Did you push him?"

"What is it with you?" She shoved him. "I'll push you."

"Stop it, guys." Ritchie grabbed Dirk's shirt when Dirk started to go after Sue Ann. "This isn't going to solve anything."

"How are we going to get to the police?" Dirk asked the first real question that needed answering.

"I can't get any signal with my CB," Ritchie said. "I've been trying since I got back here last night."

We got Mason's body on the cot he'd put in there. All of us gathered around him and looked down. I closed my eyes and wished him to be alive when I opened them. My wish wasn't granted.

"Should we say a little prayer?" I asked. "I think we need to do something."

"Fine." Mary Elizabeth always saw herself as a good Christian lady. "Everyone close your eyes." She muttered a quick prayer.

"Why would you want to hook up your CB if you didn't think you were going to use it?" Abby asked Ritchie after she must've taken the prayer's silence to think about what he'd said.

"It's always a good idea when you're out here like this to have some sort of communication with the outside world." He glared at Abby from the other side of Mason's corpse. "I look forward to when they get the asphalt down so they can bring in electric."

"Now what?" Sue Ann asked.

"We need to wait until Ritchie can get his CB up and running, or we can get out of here once all the water dries up." Agnes stomped the ground. The mud splashed up under her hiking boot. "If we don't get any more rain, this heat and humidity will help dry up the ground, hopefully let us get out of here."

"You won't be taking that big camper out of here. It'll take a few more days of no rain to drive that out through the mud." Ritchie didn't bring me any hope. "I can get people out with my truck if it gets dry enough. I guess." He looked back down at Mason. "I could put him in the bed of the truck."

"That's a plan." Agnes wrung her hands. "No one leave this camp until I say so. That includes you." She looked at Sue Ann.

"I can't stay here. My crew is back at our camp, waiting on me. They will go out and look if I don't get back." Sue Ann made a valid point.

"Then I'll talk to you first. But right now, I need to go shower." Agnes looked at Ritchie. "There's no more we can do for Mason. You and Dirk get the fire started and get to cookin'. We all need to get a little somethin' in our stomachs."

All the Laundry Club gals went back to the camper while the others did what Agnes told them.

"I've got this CB from Dottie." I retrieved the wadded-up mess of cords from the storage underneath one of the couches.

"Oh my stars." Agnes looked more scared of that than the idea of a killer among us. "That's as old as the one my Graham had."

"I don't know how to use it, but I can tell you this: we need to figure it out." When Abby held her hands out, I gave it to her.

"If we are taking handouts, I'll take my pearls now." Mary Elizabeth held her hand out to Agnes.

Abby looked up from trying to untangle the wires, and I glanced their way to see Agnes's reaction.

"You will get those back after we find out what exactly happened to Mason." Agnes carried her backpack with the pearls and whatever other evidence she had collected into the bathroom with her.

"Do you really think he was murdered?" Mary Elizabeth followed behind her.

"I think there are a lot of variables." Agnes and Mary Elizabeth stood in the hallway. "I think there are three people who weren't very happy with him. I also think he was a professional hiker and climber who just so happened to fall off a cliff that I'm sure he'd been on millions of times?"

Mary Elizabeth came back into the family room, and so did Agnes. They sat down on the couch. Abby had gotten the CB free and walked back toward the bedroom, where the radio and stereo equipment was located, plugging the CB into any hole in which it would fit.

"There weren't any cracks in the rock for him to trip. And I didn't see any puddles of water or slippery areas." I gave my observation and poured myself a cup of coffee now that it stopped brewing. "Here is what I know." I opened the kitchen junk drawer, where I had stored a notebook I'd used for other murders I'd been involved in. I took out the notebook and pen.

I walked down the hallway and gave the notebook to Abby. She set the CB on the floor and joined us in the kitchen area.

"Not that I think you did it," I stated directly at Mary Elizabeth and scratched my forearm where the chiggers had gotten me. "But I'd not be doing a good job of figuring out all the pieces unless I said this."

Mary Elizabeth uneasily shifted positions on the couch, tucking her feet up under her and nestling her hands between her legs.

"Mary Elizabeth and Mason had a lot of unkind words between them. As we now know, her pearls were stolen." I glanced over at Abby to make sure she was writing all this down and using the diagram we'd used before where we listed the victim then the suspects. Sort of like you'd see on one of those crime shows. "He had approached Mary Elizabeth about buying them. He offered a pretty penny, but she refused. He waited until we left to go look for Abby's map's treasure to break into my camper and steal them. Which he denied."

I put that in there so we'd have it documented.

"We have Sue Ann Jaffarian. His ex-girlfriend of many years, who he claimed stole his maps after he'd done generations of hard work to get to this point. He also had her kicked out of the campsite and tried to get her thrown out of the other one, creating a lot of anger in her." I paced back and forth as I dug deep into my memory for their exact conversation. "And she just so happened to show up after he fell?"

"Don't forget she did the finger-across-the-neck gesture." Agnes did the motion.

The goosebumps crawled along my neck as I watched her bony finger cross her throat.

"Oh yeah." Abby held her pen up in the air and then went back to writing. "She said she wished the curse would get him."

"Love and scorn is a good motive to kill someone," I said, rubbing my neck to take away the itching from those pesky bug bites.

"Then we have Dirk." I glanced out the kitchen window over to the headquarters tent, where Dirk still stood over the table, looking at the drawings. He had a cup of coffee in his hand.

"Dirk? That's his partner." Queenie didn't seem so convinced he could be a suspect.

"But Dirk was supposed to get fifty percent of the treasure since Sue Ann was knocked out of her percentage." I wiggled my finger in the air. "Mason told him he wasn't getting the fifty this time, and it angered Dirk. Money is a good motivator."

"What was my motive?" Mary Elizabeth asked.

"Revenge. You wanted your pearls back, and when you saw him on the rock with your pearls in his hand, you pushed him out of anger." The words rolled out of my mouth before I could stop them.

"I'll be…" She jerked, sitting up on the couch. She gave me a hard stare. "I'm going for a walk." She jumped up and headed straight out the door.

"I have lime-green nail polish." Queenie unzipped her fanny pack. "Dab a little on each one of them chigger bites. It'll kill the eggs under the skin."

"Eggs are under my skin?" The thought of little bugs hatching under my skin and living in my body was scarier than seeing Mason's corpse.

"Maybelline! Mayyyybellllieeeeen!" Mary Elizabeth's shrill voice pierced the walls of the camper from the outside while me and the other Laundry Ladies tried to figure out motive.

Nearly scalding myself with my coffee, I plunged toward the door and opened it. Mary Elizabeth stood at the entrance of the headquarters tent, screaming her head off.

Ritchie and Sue Ann were already running over to her.

"What's she's squalling about?" Agnes asked as we all piled out of the camper.

"Dirk!" Mary Elizabeth covered her mouth with her hands.

Ritchie and Sue Ann pushed past her. I ran faster and faster to see what was going on. Ritchie and Sue Ann had stopped once they got inside, but they weren't near the area where we'd placed Mason.

"Did you kill him too?" Sue Ann lunged toward Mary Elizabeth right as I got there.

"Stop it." I stood as a buffer just in time.

"Are you sure he's dead?" Agnes asked.

I glanced over at Dirk's body lying on the ground near the table where he and Mason had looked over the maps. I walked over and bent down to see if there were any signs of life. I shook my head at Agnes, signaling he was dead.

I quickly observed the bowl of stew on the ground that it appeared he had been eating. The cup of water sat on the table. It was as if he were standing over the maps, eating. The thought of how he could be doing that with Mason's body in there was just unbelievable to me.

Mary Elizabeth had started to shake. Abby wrapped her arms around her and took her out of the tent where they met Queenie. The three of them walked to the camper.

"His eyes are open. There's no pulse." Ritchie gulped. "I think he's dead."

"This is not good." Agnes's eyes shifted, but her face was still and stern. Her saggy jowls quivered. "Ritchie, how are the roads?"

"I just got back from looking, and they are still too muddy to even think about trying to move across them."

"We need to move out of the tent. This is a crime scene, as are Dirk and Mason's campers." Agnes used her arms to usher all of us out.

"It couldn't be something he ate because we've eaten all the same stuff," Ritchie suggested. "Maybe they ate some wild berries? There's no visible signs of death."

"I have to go. I can't stay here any longer." Sue Ann hugged herself. "My crew will be out looking for me, and I'm afraid I'll end up dead if I hang out here."

"I want to talk to you." Agnes was insistent Sue Ann stay.

"I don't have to…" Sue Ann started to protest before Abby saved the day.

"I got the CB to work!" Abby yelled from the open door of the camper and then ran over to us. "I got Dottie on the line, and she called the police. Hank was with her." She huffed and puffed as the adrenaline coursed through her. "They are going to use some ATVs to try to get in here."

"Abby!" I threw my arms around her. "You're a genius."

THIRTEEN

The Normal police had done one better than ATVs: they brought in the National Park Rangers and their big Jeeps. The Rangers had gone into the woods to where we told them Mason had fallen off the cliff. Agnes told them he was pushed.

"I've never been so happy to see you." I couldn't stop staring at Hank. "This has been a nightmare, and I think it's the curse you told me about."

"I'd bet there's a logical explanation for why there are two men dead." Hank stood next to me and Agnes while we watched the police start their investigation alongside the rangers.

"There is all right." Agnes gave him a swift nod. "There's a murderer here." She pointed directly at Sue Ann and Mary Elizabeth.

"Hold on. You don't know that." I sucked in a deep breath. "Agnes has deputized herself in order to investigate."

"You did?" Hank looked so pleased with his granny. She agreed with pride. "What did you find out?"

"I found out Mason wasn't very popular. Sue Ann Jaffarian is his ex who he claims stole his maps to find the treasure. If that's not enough, he had her and her crew kicked out of here and almost out of the other campsite. And it just so happened she'd come right around the corner after Mason was pushed off the cliff." Agnes's thin brows cocked up. "Then we had Dirk, but I guess he's dead and really isn't a suspect. Unless he somehow killed himself." She stopped talking, like that was a possibility.

"How is Mary Elizabeth on your list?" Hank asked in an entertaining sort of way.

"Mason kept asking to buy her pearls off of her. He was very persistent. Then, someone broke into our camper."

Agnes had told Hank too much. He looked at me with big eyes and a dropped jaw.

"It's fine." I waved my hands. "At no time were we in danger."

"We were. A killer and two dead." Agnes was good about reminding us. "Anyways, Mary Elizabeth accused him of stealing them. They were in his hand when he fell off the cliff. I put them in my bag for evidence."

"Don't forget the finger." Queenie ran a finger across her neck.

"That was Sue Ann, not Mary Elizabeth." Agnes nodded. "Yeah. Sue Ann." She made the gesture.

"Be sure you tell the police all of this." He held his hand out to shake the hand of the officer who walked up to us. "Jerry, I think you know Mae."

"Yes. Hello, Mae," he greeted me. Jerry stood about six feet tall and was probably in his sixties. A little bit of a belly showed underneath his blue uniform. He had black hair. He was nothing special like Hank. I'd seen him at the station a few times but never really talked to him. "Mae, I'm going to need the keys to your campervan. It will have to be fingerprinted because Ms. Moberly claims the pearls were stolen, and she wants to file a stolen goods report. And if this does become a homicide team, we will have to keep it here until our investigation is over."

"The campervan is open. The keys are in the console." What kind of bad luck was going on here? First Mary Elizabeth's pearls were stolen. There was a terrible rainstorm that cut us off from the world, not to mention no cell service. Then Mason died, followed up by Dirk dying, and now my home was taken from me.

I was beginning to think the curse was real, and John Swift never intended anyone to find his hidden treasure.

"How are you?" He focused his attention on Agnes. After all, she did work for the man.

"You know me." She winked. "Finer than frog's hair. But I deputized myself in order to keep this an investigation."

"You did." Jerry looked amused. "And what did you discover?"

Hank tugged me aside when Agnes started telling Jerry exactly what she'd told Hank.

"Are you okay?" Hank asked again as if I'd had a few minutes to think about it since he'd last asked.

"I'm fine. I just want to get my camper back to Happy Trails and be done with this," I told him and watched as the officers had Sue Ann and Queenie sitting on the back of the Jeep, asking them questions.

"That won't be tonight. It's too muddy out there." He ran his hand through his hair and looked at me with his big green eyes. "I knew you shouldn't've come out here. I'm glad Granny was with you."

"How's Fifi?" I asked, wanting to change the subject.

"She's fine, and you can't avoid talking about this." He wasn't going to stop poking the bear. "I mentioned bad weather. I told you there's no cell service out here. Thank God, Abby knows what she's doing."

"Are you kidding me?" I was annoyed. "It was fun until this. You can't keep me in a bubble, Hank. I live my own life."

"Yes, you do. But I'm in it now, and it's my job to protect you from the evils that can happen in and around the forest." He made it sound like a third-world country.

"Are you two arguing?" Queenie must've satisfied the officer with her answers as well as Sue Ann, because they'd been replaced by Abby and Ritchie. "Is this the first spat?" she teased.

"He's saying how it's his job to protect me. I think I did all right out here, didn't I, Queenie?" I asked her for confirmation.

"I'll let you protect me." She winked.

"You are too much." I shook my head. "When do you think I can drive out of here?"

"It might be tomorrow." He looked up, and the sun was giving its last bit of heat before it sank behind the trees for the night. "Or it could be two days. Depending on how quick it'll dry."

"I'm not staying here that long." Queenie bounced on her toes.

"No. We will take y'all out tonight." Hank rubbed his hand up and down my back.

"Hank." Jerry called Hank over. "Can I see you for a second?"

I watched as Agnes stood in between them. She was telling them something that I couldn't make out. She was talking softly, and her jowls wiggled when she nodded her head while one of the officers talked to her.

"What do you suppose she's saying?" Queenie asked me.

"I don't know." My eyes narrowed. "I have a sneaky suspicion she knows something or saw something, and she didn't tell us."

Queenie, Abby, Mary Elizabeth and I had taken turns being brought out of the campsite by a ranger on the back of an ATV to where Hank's big blue car waited on part of the new asphalt road.

"Where's Agnes?" I asked Hank when one of the rangers brought him out of the campsite. I was squeezed on the hump in the middle of the front seat with the lap belt on and Mary Elizabeth next to me. Queenie and Abby were in the back.

Hank leaned across the front seat and looked at Mary Elizabeth.

"Why aren't you in the back?" he asked her and ignored me.

"I want to be here with my daughter before someone hauls me off to jail." She patted my leg. "I'm not stupid. I know what those officers were getting at when they asked me all them questions."

"What questions?" I asked her. "You didn't kill anyone."

"You were off in the woods, peeing," Queenie reminded us.

"You peed in the woods?" Hank put the keys in the ignition and started the car. "That is out of your character."

It was out of Mary Elizabeth's southern manners to do anything of the sort, but when you gotta go, you gotta go.

"See. Right there." She turned her head and looked out of the window.

"It doesn't mean she killed Mason." I let out a long sigh and rolled my eyes. "If anyone is to be looked at, I think it'd be Sue Ann Jaffarian."

"The police will decide all of that." Hank made a U-turn and headed back to Normal.

"How is Happy Trails with all the rain?" I asked, hoping to get our minds off the murders for a little bit of time.

"It's all good. But I heard the rain devastated some of the primitive camp sites. Sue Ann told the rangers where she and her crew were staying, so they sent some other rangers there to see if they were stuck." Hank gripped the wheel. The tense jawline told me he was thinking, and I was positive it was about the murders, something I would question him about when it was just me and him.

"The dogs?" I asked, even though I'd asked earlier.

"I told you they are fine. Fifi will be happy to see you when we get back to my place." Hank glanced over and gave me a planted smile.

"She'll be staying with me." Mary Elizabeth's mouth was clenched, a sure sign she wasn't happy.

"I'm not staying with you or you," I told them both. "I've got an entire campground of rentable campers and bungalows."

"Fine." Mary Elizabeth harrumphed.

"Y'all are quiet." I turned around and looked at Abby and Queenie. Both were just staring out the window.

"I want to go home, get a good shower, and see what I missed on social media." Abby stared at the phone in her hand.

"I need some exercise to clear my head," Queenie said with quiet but desperate firmness. "I can't believe the curse has struck again."

"Oh." Abby's eyes grew. "I can hashtag the heck out of our trip and use 'swift curse' as the tag." Abby's face lit up when her phone dinged. "Whoooohooo!" There was excitement in her voice. "I've got service."

"We won't see her for a week," I joked about Abby being so tied to her social media.

"Speaking of social media. Mayor MacKenzie was in the office when Dottie got ahold of me, and she is all over this murder thing. She doesn't want anyone to say anything until the investigation is over."

Hank knew the back roads so well. He was able to get us to Happy Trails in no time.

"So it is a murder investigation." I made a point to hear him admit it.

"I'm not saying that. I'm saying that she wants to make sure before anything gets out." He never liked how I could manipulate the words that came out of his mouth.

"Looky there." Queenie sat up on the edge of the back seat and laid her elbows on the back of the front seat, staring out the windshield. "Dottie is wearing the soles of her shoes out from pacing."

The grass in front of Dottie's camper was all patted down where it looked like she'd been walking back and forth. Dottie must've heard us driving up the gravel because she stood there with her hands on her hips, pink sponge curlers in her hair and a cigarette dangling from her lips.

She waved her arms in the air, and her eyes were half closed as the smoke billowed in her face.

"Wait!" she hollered when Hank almost passed her up.

He brought the car to an abrupt stop, and everyone but him opened their doors.

"We'll walk from here." I gave him a quick kiss on the cheek. "I'll be down to get Fifi."

"I can drop her off. And Chester, if you don't mind." There was that look on his face again, the look that told me he was going to be working on this case and there wouldn't be any time for us.

"So it is an investigation." I eyed him when all the gals were out of earshot and trying to tell Dottie their side of the story.

"It's suspicious. That's all. And they need all the manpower they can get. I'm going to be looking into a few things for them while they process the scene. The rangers are involved too." He shrugged. "I'm not sure how involved I'll be or how much they're going to need me, but I'm only working on one other case that doesn't even have to do with the John Swift silver mines."

"I'd love to keep Chester. Does that mean you won't be back tonight?" I asked.

"Probably not." He put his hand on the side of my face. "I'm glad you're okay. When Dottie called, I got scared."

"I'm fine," I said just as Dottie tapped on Hank's window.

He rolled it down.

"You're staying with me tonight. We can get Joel Grassel to get in Ritchie's campsite tomorrow and tow you out if we need to." Dottie showed no signs of relenting. Her words were final.

"I can stay in one of the unrented campers." I shook my head. "I don't need to be a bother to anyone."

"Unrented?" She laughed. "Honey, when the rain fell, all those campsite people came here to stay. We are booked solid. Get out of the car and grab a shower. I've got some grub on over at the main campfire. You come on over and get something good in your belly."

"You heard the woman," I said to Hank. "I'll grab the dogs soon."

After we kissed goodbye and got out of the car, Dottie leaned over and whispered, "Uh-oh." She lifted her chin at the car pulling in. "Here comes trouble."

Mayor Courtney MacKenzie drove by real slow, curling her finger at me to come see her.

She parked her car near the office, which was right across from Dottie's camper. She got out, and before she headed toward me, I went ahead and met her there. Dottie had rejoined Queenie, Abby, and Mary Elizabeth in front of her place.

"What went on out there?" the mayor asked me.

"Good evening." I took the moment to greet her. "I'm doing fine."

"I know you're fine, Mae. You're always fine. But if you want to do the pleasantries, how are you really?" She drawled with distinct mockery.

"I'm starving, and I need a shower." I pointed to the communal campfire. "I… um…"

"What?" the mayor asked when it was apparent that I'd totally lost my train of thought as I saw Sue Ann Jaffarian and her crew grabbing some of the food.

"I'm not sure what went on out there. Like I told the police, we were hiking, and all of a sudden Mason fell from the sky. After that, we got him out of there, and the next thing we knew, Dirk, his partner, was also dead." I shrugged. "I'm thinking they ate some poisonous berries because they aren't from here."

"Really?" She eyed me. "As experienced as they were?" she asked but continued yammering on. "This isn't going to look good and keep people from coming to find the treasure. I've spent a lot of time and effort getting those gravel roads paved with asphalt. It wasn't easy. There were many things I had to do besides go to Frankfort and lobby for the grants. I had to go to the gaming commission, the National Parks commission, and the agriculture commission."

"I'm sure you went through a lot, but I can't help that this happened." I wasn't really sure what she wanted me to do.

"You can help keep this on the down low with all the campers who have decided to stay here. If they hear these people could've possibly been murdered, they will hightail it out of here, thinking the locals are killing off people for the silver just like they did over at the Red River Gorge some years back."

I had no idea what she was talking about. But I nodded my head anyways.

The Red River Gorge I did know. It was a very popular hiking area some bit away from Normal. But the locals? That was nothing I knew about.

"And her." She jerked a look at Abby. "Tell her to stop posting stuff. Making us look bad. I'll be in touch with you later."

I wanted to ask her why she would need to be in touch with me, but she jumped back in her car and sped off.

"What was that about?" Dottie asked with the girls all waiting for my answer after I walked back over to them.

"I have no idea." I shook my head. "Something about she's gone to great lengths to get the asphalt and promote the Swift mine and for you to stop your attacks against it on social media."

"She called my tweets attacks?" Abby snarled and threw her stare at the entrance of Happy Trails Campground.

"She said something about the Gorge." I laughed. "We can revisit all this tomorrow. Why don't we grab some food so we can all get a good night's sleep?"

"And meet up at the Laundry Club in the morning?" Mary Elizabeth asked.

We all looked at each other and grinned. It was the unsaid agreement we all understood. If there were murders to be solved, and one of us was a suspect, the only place we wanted to be was the laundromat.

Mary Elizabeth, Abby, and Queenie walked up to where my campervan was supposed to be parked, jumped into their parked cars, and headed out of the campground.

I grabbed my phone and quickly texted Dawn Gentry, honorary Laundry Club lady and the co-owner of the

Milkery with Mary Elizabeth, to give her a quick update about what had transpired with Mary Elizabeth. I also told her to keep an eye on Mary Elizabeth since they lived together and to call me no matter what time it was if she needed me.

Her reply: *You've got to be kidding me. I'll call you in the morning.*

I replied to her text: *Meet us at the Laundry Club at eight a.m. if you can make it.*

"What on earth happened out there?" Dottie asked on our way over to Hank's camper to get the dogs. "The girls told me, but you know how they all see things so differently."

Dottie Swaggert wasn't fooling me at all. She loved to gossip just as much as the rest of the Laundry Club ladies.

"Do you really think Mary Elizabeth did it? I mean, according to Queenie, she's not sure who killed him, but she did say she couldn't get Mary Elizabeth's actions out of her head." Was Dottie telling me that Queenie thought Mary Elizabeth could possibly have killed Mason?

"No." I shook my head. "Mason really flirted with her, and she really was buying it until he offered to give her money for the pearls. Then she told him they were passed down from her great-grandmother. He was practically salivating from the mouth."

Why was I finding myself completely defending Mary Elizabeth when I shouldn't even respond to such ridiculous accusations?

"Mae, according to Abby, Mary Elizabeth had decided to go to the woods to use the bathroom. That's completely out of her nature. Then Mason falls to his death? She walks back around to y'all and immediately goes to grab her pearls out of Mason's hand? That was her first reaction?" Dottie's words made my insides curl with fright.

"Did they really tell you all that? Because it sure does sound like they all believe Mary Elizabeth killed him." It was not sitting right with me to think our friends would truly believe she'd kill him. "What about Sue Ann Jaffarian?"

"I'm just saying, according to…" she started again.

"According to who? According to what?" I rolled my eyes. "I don't want to hear any more." Then I had a disturbing thought. "Did they tell the police all this?"

Dottie shrugged and stood on the outside of Hank's camper while I reached up and opened the door. Fifi and Chester bolted out, focusing on Dottie.

"Fifi," I called my little white furball and bent down. When she heard my voice, she darted over to me. "My sweet girl. Mama missed you."

Fifi danced with delight in circles and tried to give me kisses on each twirl. Chester nearly bowled her over, getting to me and almost knocking me down. He was a lot stouter than my little poodle.

"They missed you so much." Dottie patted me on the shoulder. "I even missed you."

"Awww. Dottie Swaggert, you do love me." I stood up and gave her a hug. "But I'm going to tell you Mary Elizabeth didn't kill anyone."

"According to…" she started again. I glared at her. "Mary Elizabeth is the number-one suspect."

FOURTEEN

It didn't take a genius to know Mary Elizabeth would likely be considered a suspect, but being the number-one suspect was far from ideal.

Dottie and the dogs took a walk around the campground to make sure everyone was settled. I took the moment to call Hank. There were some questions I wanted to ask him. When the call went straight to voicemail, I figured he'd gone back to the campsite to help out and didn't have cell service.

"Are you doing okay?" I'd decided to stop at the communal campfire, where Dottie and Hank had prepared the skillet hamburger casserole, which was a very inexpensive campfire supper when you needed to feed the masses.

"We are fine." Sue Ann Jaffarian had a big plate of food and a bottle of beer. She didn't look a bit upset or even fazed about being a suspect. "I just wish Mason and

Dirk were here too." She put down her plate and picked up the bottle.

I sat down in the chair next to her. This was my time to ask her any questions that could help out Mary Elizabeth.

"Mason and I had some ups and downs. Currently on a down, but we would've gotten over it." She took a swig of her beer and leaned back in the chair. "Mason was so focused on finding the treasure, he got sloppy. I told him that one day he was going to be so unfocused that he was going to slip up." Her eyes teared.

"I'm sorry. I know you must've truly loved him." I tried to be as empathetic as I could, since I was trying to get something on her for the police to focus on and take some heat off of Mary Elizabeth. "What map was Mason talking about?"

"Map? What map?" she asked.

"When we questioned Mason why he made you leave the campsite, he said it was because you'd stolen his maps, and it was obvious because you were at the same treasure site as the map." I might've stretched the truth. That was what we politely called a lie. Mason didn't say all of that, but he did imply it. At least, in my opinion he implied she was there because of that specific map.

"The map I took was a map of all the campsites in the area. It didn't have anything to do with the John Swift treasure." She jerked her backpack up from the ground and unzipped it, tumbling some of the contents out of it.

Mainly it was Ziploc baggies of food like the kind Mason had given us. I bent down and picked some of them up. I understood the granola and nuts for energy, but the salad was beyond my comprehension.

"Salad?" I asked when she stuffed them back in her bag and dug around for something else.

"Yeah." She snickered. "I have to keep my bowels moving." She rolled her eyes and continued to dig in the backpack.

"Most of the primitive campsites aren't listed on the National Park's registry." She took out a piece of paper, and in exchange for the Ziplocs, she handed me the map. "I'm the one who made the map as we stayed at these places. He didn't want me to have what was rightly mine. I didn't need his help in trying to find different spots to look within the forest. Those places are documented all over the John Swift journal entries and other treasure hunters who've come before us."

I looked at the paper. It was an outline of the Daniel Boone National Forest with several Xs dotted around with the names of the campsites. A few I'd recognized from just hearing around town or the hikers who would come through the trails that lead into Happy Trails, but most of them I didn't even know existed.

"Can I get a copy of this?" I asked.

"You can have that one. I made several copies just in case Mason tried to sneak into my camper and steal it. He was very sneaky." Her voice choked. There were tears in her eyes. "We had some really good times until he got so greedy and wanted to cut me out. I wish I could take back the last time I saw him."

"You mean the fight?" I asked.

"Yeah…" she trailed off. "I only wished I was able to confront Dirk like I wanted to."

"Dirk?" I questioned.

"He and Mason were in the final stages of their collaboration. After I left, Mason told Dirk he'd give him half of the treasures found. Dirk had been waiting a long time to replace me, and he'd spent the better part of the last year doing all the research for this trip." She wiped away a tear that'd fallen down her cheek.

"I heard them arguing in the tent," I told her. "He was saying how Mason had gone back on the percentage." I didn't tell her all of the conversation I'd overheard, since it was something I needed to tell Hank now that I remembered that little piece of their argument.

"They were fighting?" Her chin dropped to her chest. "I told Mason not to mess around with lies. But he thought he could just throw his weight around like he was the only one who could find any treasure, no matter where we went on hunts. I just couldn't take his greediness anymore."

"So you broke up with him?" I asked.

"Yeah." Her head jerked up, her brows furrowing. "Did you think differently?"

"I wasn't sure when he talked about you. It was never clear." I sucked in a deep breath and pushed myself up to stand. "It's been a long couple of days, and I'm going to head on to bed. Let me know if you or any of your crew need anything."

"Thanks, Mae. I'm sorry your mom is wrapped up in all this, but I truly think Dirk did it. He had motive, and I'm not so sure he didn't end his own life." Her words made my stomach clench tight.

Dirk and Mason did have a fight. It was about money. Like Sue Ann said, Mason was greedy, and ultimately, was that what got him killed? How did Dirk die?

All of these were questions that would need time, and maybe a good night's sleep would bring me some clarity, plus give the police enough time to get some preliminary answers.

FIFTEEN

It was too bad I let Hank live in one of the nicer campervans I had to offer for guests. There were different levels of camping in Happy Trails and different ways to camp. I was so happy to have been able to offer some campervans where campers could actually rent them and drive them in and around the Daniel Boone National Park.

When Hank had moved in, renting actual campervans was a new concept Abby Fawn had started to market for me on behalf of Happy Trails. I never figured it'd be one of the hotter commodities with guests. Now, we had a long line of reservations, and Hank taking one of them up wasn't helping out my bottom dollar, but it did make me happy he was here.

The inside of the van was perfect for a couple of people. The two captain's chairs in the front did turn around. There was a small table with two built-in bench chairs on either side. Across was the kitchenette with a two-burner stove, a small oven, and a microwave built into the storage cabinets above. In the back of the van was a full-sized queen mattress and not more than a closet-sized bathroom with a handheld shower.

When Joel Grassel had found it and sold it to me, my foster brother Bobby Ray and I had gone to great lengths to clean it up and get it all ready. Since Bobby Ray was the best mechanic in all of Kentucky, he had the thing purring like it was brand new. We'd laid in a new wood floor, and I'd gotten new white cabinets and butcher block counter tops. The table was also made of butcher block, with blue accents. The light colors made the campervan feel larger than it really was, and there was plenty of storage.

Hank didn't drive it as it was meant to be, and since the dogs and I had slept there last night, I found it to be a lot more comfortable than I'd expected.

Instead of making coffee or even walking over to the guests next door to grab a cup of joe from their early-morning campfire, I'd decided to head on into Normal and get a cup of coffee from The Trails Coffee Shop. I was going to meet the gals at the Laundry Club anyways, and Dottie was already working for me, since I was still supposed to be on the treasure hunt. I wasn't going to waste my morning.

Besides, I was a little antsy to see if Hank had heard anything about how Dirk had died. If it was a case of death by his own hand, Mason's murder could be solved and shut, which meant Mary Elizabeth was completely off the hook.

"You two stay here." I put some kibble in Fifi's and Chester's bowls after I let them back in from doing their business. "I hope we get our home back today." I gave Fifi a good scratch on the ear, grabbed my bag, and headed out the door to get into my car.

It wasn't any sort of lavish car. Again, Joel Grassel had it on the lot when I'd first rolled into town, and when it became very apparent I wasn't leaving Normal anytime soon, it was much easier to buy a cheap car, because that was all I could afford, and keep the campervan parked at the campground.

My mind was so occupied with what Sue Ann had told me. It was a shame I wasn't taking in the gorgeous scenery. About this time every year, and under the right conditions, dogwoods and sumacs turned red and purple, sugar maples turned orange and red, oaks, sourwoods and sweet gums took on red hues, and poplars and hickories turned yellow and gold. It was truly a spectacular real-life painting.

One-way roads ran down Main Street, with a grassy median between them. It wasn't just any median. It was one where people gathered at the picnic tables that stood among the large oak trees on each side of an amphitheater and covered seating area. Thick white pillars you'd see on the front porch of a plantation home held up the structure. Each post had a real gas lantern hanging off it. Large ferns toppled over several ceramic planters. There were twinkling lights around each pole, giving it such a romantic feel.

There were little shops that ran along each side of Main Street. They ranged from the Smelly Dog, which was a pet groomer, to the Normal Diner, the Tough Nickel Thrift Shop, and Deter's Feed-N-Seed, along with more boutique-type shops that I couldn't wait to check out. The display windows of each shop even had visions of family camping and summers in Normal—as well as the much-needed Trails Coffee Shop, which was where I had my eyes set on.

All the shops were free-standing cottage-style homes with a small courtyard between them. Today, there were some open tables at the Trails Coffee Shop, perfect for me to sit and enjoy my first cup of the day.

"It's a little early for you." Gert Hobson was the owner of the coffee shop. "Did you not get your order? That new delivery guy is about to get delivered some firing." She shook her head.

"No." I waved my hands in front of me to stop her blood pressure from rising. "I'm sure your coffee is there. I'm not working today so I decided to come into town early and enjoy a nice cup of coffee right here."

I had an agreement with many of the local businesses in Normal. I only used their products in my campground. I served complimentary coffee from Gert alongside the Cookie Crumbles' donuts, or scones or muffins in the recreational center at the campground. The guests were also offered many different baskets to purchase with various local goodies in them. For instance, if they wanted more coffee, for a small fee they could purchase a coffee basket that featured Gert's specialty coffees and treats. If they wanted a spa kit, which were very popular with the girls' weekends, they could purchase a basket put together from Cute-icles. It was my way of giving back to Normal after what my ex-and-now-dead-husband, Paul, had done to the town. In turn and just because the people in Normal are good, the area businesses put Happy Trails Campground flyers in their shops and even in customers' bags.

It truly was an amazing community, and I was proud to now call it home.

"Well." She smacked her hands together. "You're in for a real treat being this early." A huge smile curled up on the edges of her lips. "I'm in there right now trying a new hot brew that I'm going to feature for Christmas."

"Christmas?" I jerked back, giving her an are-you-crazy look.

"Now, don't be looking at me all googly eyed. When you own a coffee shop, you have to think a few months ahead so you can create the perfect holiday blend." Swiftly she turned around and stopped at the door. "What are you waiting for? Christmas?" she laughed. "Get on in here."

Gert had really taken the name to a whole 'nother level inside. There were café tables inside as well as long farm tables. In the middle of the tables, she'd repurposed old bourbon barrel lids and made really cool lazy Susans out of them. Each one had little containers of different condiments you'd need for any type of coffee. It was like each table had its own little coffee bar that could just be twirled around to make the perfect cup of coffee.

One of the walls was a living wall. She'd had some fancy architet come in and design it especially for the shop using only the plants, flowers, and greenery local to the Daniel Boone National Forest. It was pretty neat.

"I just love it in here." I continued to look around while she got my special coffee ready to sample. "Is it busy like this all the time?"

I moved to the far end of the counter so her employees could wait on the already-long line of customers so early in the morning.

"They all like to get a head start on most of the trails before it gets too hot or crowded." She pushed all sorts of buttons on a fancy machine, and then she stirred and crushed up some beans. I watched in awe as she created something that was in her head without reading from a piece of paper.

She looked extremely busy at the moment, so I took the opportunity to walk around and check out some of the local items posted on her corkboard. Most of the business had a corkboard on the wall, showing the different things going on in the amphitheater or just around Normal. The John Swift flyer stood out the most. It was from Ritchie's campsite. He was offering a discount if you stayed at his place, something I either had no idea about or had taken advantage of automatically, since he'd immediately asked for the cash after we parked. Then I wondered if I could get my money back since we didn't stay, but it wasn't that much, so I just put that out of my mind and moved on to the next bulletin on the corkboard.

It was from the National Forestry and Rangers in the Daniel Boone National Forest. It had a picture of a five-leaf plant that looked like poison ivy, and in bold red ink it read ALERT.

That got my attention.

No one wants to get poison ivy on any sort of trail. Henry was great about getting it all chopped down at the beginning of the trails that led in and out of Happy Trails because I didn't want any of my campground guests having to deal with that.

I read, "In an effort to increase wild ginseng populations on national forest lands, a ban prohibiting ginseng harvest in the Daniel Boone National Forest has been extended through the harvest season, from Sept. 1 to Dec. 1."

Ginseng? I took another look at the leafy plant they'd displayed underneath the big red alert.

I continued to read: *"It's illegal to harvest any ginseng," Forest Supervisor Ken Bailey said. "Only Kentucky licensed dealers can legally export ginseng out of Kentucky, and it must be accompanied by appropriate documents. A harvester may apply to become a dealer to certify one's own roots. Diggers, this includes mailing your ginseng to an out-of-state dealer, leaving the state post-harvest, or meeting with an out-of-state dealer by vehicle. Kentucky ginseng cannot legally leave the borders of Kentucky without an export certificate issued by our agency."*

I reread the quote. I'd never even known ginseng was a thing in the forest.

"The forest stopped issuing ginseng collecting permits in an attempt to boost the plant's population in the forest due to years of noticeable ginseng decline across the forest. Remember you have to have a legal permit to even harvest ginseng." The article continued with a statement from Ken Bailey. *"This year those permit holders are on suspension, and there will be no harvesting this season. If you do and are caught, you will be prosecuted. There is a hefty fine and a minimum prison sentence starting at six years."*

"Mae, your coffee is ready," I heard Gert say.

After I scanned down the rest of the article, I went to get the fancy coffee where she'd designed a Christmas tree, of all things, in the foam.

"Seriously?" I questioned her with half a smile. "The last thing I want to think about is Christmas. It's my least busy time, and I generally have to take a job with Betts Hager in her cleaning service to make ends meet. Though I'm really working hard at trying to save any extra money at the campground so we don't have many lean months."

"The campground is rocking. You're doing amazing things still." She was referring to the key I'd gotten from Mayor MacKenzie a few months back after I'd helped improve the region's economy by upgrading the campground and adding all the new features that really made camping a lot more glamorous than it had been in years.

"Thanks. It's just that everyone wants to hibernate in the winter and not take hiking trips." I picked up the ceramic mug, lifted it to my lips, and took a little sip. I closed my eyes and let the warm, cozy peppermint-infused liquid slide down my throat. "It sure does taste like Christmas." I licked my lips and took another sip. "Any chances I can get this in a to-go cup? I have to meet some of the gals at the Laundry Club this morning."

"I'll make all of them a cup." Gert winked and headed back to her fancy equipment, where she started that whole process all over again.

I took the mug over to a little table out of the way of the other customers, sat in the café table near the corkboard, and snapped a photo of the alert from the forestry department.

I texted Dottie: *Have you heard of this crazy ginseng thing?*

Dottie texted back: *Big business if you are one of the lucky ones to get a permit.*

I texted back: *Do you have a permit? Or know of anyone who has one?*

Dottie texted back: *Nope. But I know plenty of people who do it illegally. Why? You need some?*

I texted: *No! I don't even know what ginseng does.*

Dottie texted a laughing emoji due to my ignorance. But with a quick internet search on my phone, it was easy enough to find out that Kentucky was a huge ginseng importer to Japan. Ginseng was claimed to help boost energy, lower blood sugar and cholesterol levels, reduce stress, promote relaxation, treat diabetes, and manage sexual dysfunction in men, which seemed like it was good for everyone.

I just might need to check into being a harvester myself. That might bring in enough money for future winters, now that Gert had that in my head.

"Here you go." Gert walked over with the cardboard coffee holder filled with the to-go cups. "If you need more, let me know. I'll have them right over."

"Thanks, Gert." I stood up and sucked down the last little bit from my mug. "You're so kind. The ladies are going to love this. Thank you."

"You seem awful interested in the ginseng poster." She took the pin out of the paper and held it out. "I've got plenty more back there to replace it. They give me stacks so people don't rip one down."

"I had no idea this was a thing." I was still in a bit of a shock.

"Crazy. People think all us locals born and bred here grow marijuana and all sorts of illegal things on the forest since it'd be so hard to track, but it's the ginseng that's so widely and worldly in demand that no one really outside of the forest knows about." She laughed.

"Maybe I can become a harvester to help supplement the income in the winter I was telling you about." I shrugged and put the paper in my bag, making sure to steady the coffee carrier.

"Not this year or you'll get thrown in the pokey," she joked on my way out the door.

SIXTEEN

"Coffee!" I hollered over at Abby, Queenie, and Betts Hager as I backed in the door, rear first, in hopes they'd run over and help me with the door or take the coffees from me.

No chance. The three of them sat on the couch in the family room area of the Laundry Club, glued to the television. But Agnes Swift had just walked out of the bathroom and hurried over to help.

"What are you doing here?" I asked, surprised to see her.

"I stopped by to check on you before I headed back to work." She was so sweet and kind.

We walked over to the group.

"I'm fine." I was going to tell her more, but the others were annoyed.

"Shhh! Hank is doing a press conference." Queenie and the other two didn't even look my way.

"Why is Hank doing the press conference?" I asked and shuffled over, careful not to spill the coffee.

Like vultures, they each grabbed a cup and sat back down. Abby picked up the remote and turned the volume up, her rude way of telling me to be quiet.

"If anyone was hiking during these hours around the Furnace, please contact the Normal Police Station. Even if you didn't see Mason Cavanaugh or Dirk Ivy. Any and all information is collected, and the slightest thing might be able to help bring us closure about what happened to these two hikers." Hank was looking directly into the camera. "Thank you."

"Oh my stars," Betts Hager gasped, making her bangs fly to the side of her forehead. She pushed back a strand of her wavy brown hair and curled her leg up under her other leg, nestling the coffee in both hands. "I tell all the kids at the church to be careful during any hikes because all experienced hikers can have accidents."

Betts was very active in our local church, Normal Baptist Church. In fact, in a former life, which we didn't talk about much, she was the preacher's wife. Though her ex was no longer the preacher or even in Normal, Betts kept an active role there and really enjoyed working with the youth. She did work with the prisoners in one of Kentucky's state prisons. After a twist of events, she changed her ministry focus to the youth program. She'd been really good at it too.

"What is going on?" I was so confused.

"They confirmed Mason died from his fall, and Dirk died of a heart attack. Hank said he'd interviewed other hikers, meaning us, along with local Ritchie Stinnett. Ritchie said he saw Sue Ann and Dirk talking at his campsite during the time it was confirmed Mason had died. He said he overheard Dirk tell Sue Ann something about Mason trying to find the treasure at the Furnace when she told him Mason cleared her team to go there. Dirk and Sue Ann took off on the trail to find him," Agnes said.

"That's why Sue Ann was there. And I found Dirk at the mouth of the cave. He said Mason was in there, but I told him he wasn't." I was glad the initial reports came back that the deaths were from natural causes because Normal didn't need any more murders.

I opened my bag and took out a paper, putting it on the coffee table.

"Here is the map Sue Ann supposedly took from Mason. It was her own map that he didn't want to give her.

She broke up with him. So now that we know Hank has apparently cleared her as a suspect, then we can too."

Abby leaned over and took the paper from the table. "What is this?" she asked and turned it around.

"Sorry. Wrong paper." I dug back in my bag and took out the map.

Agnes picked it up and looked at it. "I'll take it with me and make us copies at work." Agnes made a good suggestion, since I guessed we were all treasure hunters together. "Speaking of work. I've got to hit it." She folded up the paper and said her goodbyes.

"What was that other paper?" Abby asked once we settled back into our little group and enjoyed our coffee.

"I might just become a ginseng harvester. I saw that on Gert's corkboard. I had no idea it was a big deal around here." I gave Abby the flyer I'd taken from the Trails Coffee Shop corkboard.

"It's a huge deal. You wouldn't believe how strict they are on the whole thing. If you can get a license to harvest, I'd love to be an employee and work for you." Betts made it clear by her statement how difficult it must be to get that license.

I've never been deterred by hard work.

"Anyways, do you have the notebook?" I asked Abby about the notebook I generally kept in my camper, which was still stuck at the campsite, where we always wrote down different ideas and clues about the other murders and crimes that we'd decided to investigate.

On our own, of course.

"Yep." She reached down and pulled it from her purse. "You can put it back in your campervan."

I took it from her and put it in my bag along with the map Sue Ann had given me.

"Maybe when Sue Ann and her crew leave, we can use her map to look for the treasure." I wiggled my brows, still very interested in finding the treasure.

"Do you think Mary Elizabeth will be up for it?" Queenie laughed. "She sure did not understand how we didn't have electric."

Abby and Queenie spoke over each other, telling Betts how uncomfortable Mary Elizabeth had been when she realized it was primitive camping.

"Mary Elizabeth." My phone rang. "Speak of the devil." I showed the three of them the screen of my phone with Mary Elizabeth's name scrolling across. "I hope you got some good sleep last night," I answered the phone.

"Listen to me. The police said I can come get my pearls." She talked about how she wanted them back and attached around her neck as soon as she could.

She yammered on about how she felt naked without them while a text from Hank came through saying my campervan had been released, and he'd take me to the campsite to pick it up.

"I'm heading to the station to get a ride to the campsite now that Hank has cleared the deaths as due to natural causes and released the campsite." Inwardly, I groaned, wondering if they had used fingerprint powder all over my home and how much time I would have to spend cleaning it up.

"You don't mind?" Her southern voice dripped through the phone. "I'd be ever so grateful. We are so busy here, and I don't want to leave Dawn alone again."

"No problem, as long as you have me over for supper." My hint wasn't so subtle, but I knew if I had to clean my campervan, the last thing I wanted to do was to cook supper.

"Supper it is. And you can invite your cute boyfriend too." Mary Elizabeth giggled and hung up the phone.

"Since we don't have any murders to investigate, I guess I'll be heading over to the station and have Hank drive me to get my campervan." I gathered all my things and made sure everything was in my bag.

"I guess I can go to the library and cut my vacation off short." Abby grabbed her phone. "Hashtag hikers beware of dangers even if you are experienced. Hashtag even experts die." She continued to ramble on as she typed on her social media about the press conference Hank had given and the findings.

"I'm going to head on over to the Normal Baptist Church undercroft to teach." Queenie adjusted her leg warmers before she stood up. "I had a student teaching today, but since I won't be wearing my sleuthing headband, I might's well get my sweat on."

"What about you?" I asked Betts.

"I've got some paperwork to catch up on and get some activities ready for youth group tonight." She sighed. "I am relieved everything is all good and no murderers on the loose."

"Yeah." I laughed and headed back to the door. "Me too!"

SEVENTEEN

The police station was a little bit outside downtown in the business district. The white courthouse was the tallest building and right in the middle. The police station was attached to the courthouse. The line of police cars was parked on the side like always.

I headed through the door, and instead of the quiet I normally heard when I visited, there was a lot of chattering and moving around in the entrance, where there was another door that actually led into the police station. Agnes was sitting on her perch behind the sliding glass window with her head down.

"Can I help you?"

The nameplate on the other side of the glass had Agnes engraved across the brass plate, and I ran my finger across it.

"I said, can I help you?" She finally looked up at me. "Mae, get on in here." She waved me to the door, where I heard it buzz to unlock. "I haven't had time to make copies of the map for our group."

"No problem. It's busy in here this morning," I said to her and looked around.

"They've been working on a big case and pulling all sorts of hikers and campers in here to question." She smacked her hands together and got off her stool, giving me a hug. "I hear you get your home back."

"I do. Where is Hank?" I asked.

"Oh dear." There was a worried look on her face. "He did mention something about you coming here when I first walked in, but I forgot what he told me to tell you. I was so busy getting some warrants ready to send over to the judge, then the mayor called all up in arms wanting to talk to Jerry, that I plumb didn't listen to a word that boy told me to tell you."

"It's all right. I'll just go look for him." It wasn't something I was used to with Hank. He'd tell me one thing, then get dragged elsewhere by work.

"He ain't here. He had to go out on the investigation he's been working on." She frowned. "Can I help you?"

"He was going to take me to get my van." Not that I expected Agnes to do anything, but I did want my house back.

She looked up at the clock and back at me.

"Listen, it's only eleven, but I was taking lunch anyways because Precious is at the Smelly Dog, getting a cut. I was going to go get her and take her home because I just hate having her stay there all day long. It just frightens her so much." Agnes referred to one of Fifi's puppies, which she'd had with Roscoe the bulldog. "You know I can't turn down those free haircuts."

Ethel Biddle, owner of the Smelly Dog Groomer, and Roscoe had felt so bad about Roscoe taking away Fifi's pristine accreditation that she offered Fifi and Roscoe's offspring free grooming for life. Hank had given one of the puppies to Agnes, and Precious was much loved.

"If you don't mind me running her home, I can drive you out to the campsite. I'm not sure what you'd do with your car here, but at least you'd have your home back." She made a great point and one I didn't want to refuse.

"Perfect. When can you leave?" I asked. There was no sense in dilly-dallying around all day when I could be at the campground with Dottie so we could get the rentals ready for the next group of guests.

"I can go now and be back by one." She reached up to the window and clicked the lock, grabbed her little pocketbook, and gestured for us to go out the back door.

"I can get Hank to drive me here to get the car anytime." I followed behind Agnes to the back door, where the employees and police cars were parked.

"What did you think about Colonel Holz's preliminary autopsy?" Agnes asked on our way back to town, where the groomer was located.

"I'm glad there isn't a murderer out there. But there were still so many people who wanted Mason dead that it's hard to believe he slipped." But who was I to go against what Mason's body had told Colonel Holz's autopsy report?

Colonel Holz was the doctor and the coroner, so he'd know like he always did.

"I told Hank I just couldn't believe how Mason had fallen. If I'd not seen it with my own eyes, maybe, but the way he fell"—she shook her head—"didn't sit well with my soul."

She found a parking spot right up in front of the Smelly Dog Groomer and turned the car off.

"You comin'?" she asked.

"I was going to stay in the car." I didn't see a reason for me to go in with her.

"Hodge-podge. Come on in and say hi to Ethel." She got out and shut the door, waiting on the sidewalk for me to get out.

"I guess I'm going," I muttered to myself and unbuckled the seat belt.

"It's good manners to say hello. And just too dang hot to stay in a car." She shuffled to the door, and I reached around her to open it.

We were greeted with the sounds of buzzing hair dryers, dogs barking, dogs whining, and a whiff of dog shampoo.

"Hey there." Orlene Roth, the young girl behind the counter, had a big grin on her burnt face. Her hair was pulled up into a high ponytail, and it swung as she talked. "Oh, Mae, we don't have Fifi."

"I'm here with Agnes." Agnes had already walked over to the door with the Employees Only sign and walked through. "She's just made herself at home."

"You know Agnes." Orlene winked. She worked here during the summer when she was on school break. I'd gotten to know her when I was doing a little substituting at the high school. "She just does whatever it is she wants to do."

Boy, was I glad that gig was over.

"You been to the beach?" I asked Orlene and walked over to the corkboard to see if Ethel had any good specials I could pass along to my camper guests. A lot of hikers and campers had animals. Some of the full-time RVers would make appointments when they did long stops to get their animals groomed.

"Nah. It's fake." She shrugged. "My mama tells me not to lie in them tanning beds, but when I go to Sally Ann Dean over at the Cute-icles, I just can't help but hop right on into the bed for a quick glow."

The employee door opened, and out ran Precious with no leash.

"Precious." I bent down and called for the little squirt. After she heard me, she ran over and jumped into my lap, ready for some good kisses. "You are so cute," I gushed over Fifi's little baby girl.

Even though Roscoe and Fifi were an unlikely pair, they sure did make some cute pups.

"I reckon you're ready." Agnes came out with the purse swinging by her side. "Anything new on the board?" Agnes asked and looked at the advertisements.

"Did you see this?" I asked her about the same notice the National Forestry had put out about the ginseng.

"That's big business around here." Agnes did a quick search of the board before she turned around to leave. "See you, Orlene. Tell your mama and them I asked about them."

I held on to Precious since it seemed Agnes didn't bring her a leash and walked out with her. Once we got into the car, I put Precious in the back, but she jumped right back up in front after I'd put my seatbelt back on.

"That ginseng thing." I adjusted in my seat so Precious could have a little more room. She looked like Fifi but was the size of Roscoe the bulldog. "I think I might just see if I can be a harvester."

Agnes shifted in her seat and gripped the wheel. She was eerily silent.

"What's wrong?" I asked and held on as she sped out of downtown onto the windy road that led to Ritchie Stinnett's campsite.

"Nothin'," she said, but I knew something was bugging her.

"I know you better than that." I eyed her suspiciously and held on to Precious for dear life. "Plus, you're a little heavy footed." I referred to her driving.

"You need to talk to Hank about the harvesting. He knows a lot more about that than I do. So before you do anything, you talk to him." She slowed the car down when the big orange triangle signs signaling road construction started popping up every few feet. "Do you hear me?"

"Yeah. Yeah." I was a bit taken aback by her adamant attitude where she just didn't want to talk about it. "I was just going to ask you about it."

"Don't." The tops of her wrinkly hands were white from how hard she was holding on to the wheel. "I'll quickly drop you off so I can get Precious home."

"Did I do something to offend you?" I questioned. "Because if I did, I'd like to know. You know me. I own up to my misgivings, and I'm not about to let another second go by without knowing what's crawled up in you and died."

So there might've been a smidgen of a lack of respect for Agnes Swift at this moment, but I wouldn't keep going and thinking I'd done something when I clearly had not. If Hank's family had said something to her to make her change her mind about our relationship, then I wanted to know. It was no secret they weren't very happy he'd moved off their property and come to live in my campground. In fact, his own mama said it was like he moved in with me, which was a big no-no around these parts before you were married. When I denied that false statement she made, she said living in the same campground was pert near the same thing.

"I've got a lot on my mind. There ain't nothing crawled up in me." She looked around. "Woooweee, this new asphalt sure is nice. I do hope the mayor gets exactly what she thinks she's gonna get because she did have a lot of the ginseng fields taken out."

"Now you want to talk about ginseng?" I was so confused. Was Agnes starting to lose it? She was eighty years old, and sometimes the mind went.

"Nope. I'm just saying these asphalt roads sure have people up in arms since it's taken a lot more land than originally anticipated with the grant." Agnes wanted to tell me something, and she was doing a terrible job covering it up.

"Spill it," I told her and waved when the road crew let us pass where the gravel road picked up.

"What?" she asked all innocent, as much as an eighty-year-old woman who loved to speak her mind could. She took two fingers and twisted them in front of her lips like she was locking something. "Tick a lock."

"Mmm-hhmmm. I'll get it out of you." I had to smile at her. She was so cute, and I adored her as much as Hank did.

For the next few minutes, I sat back and closed my eyes to let the sunshine peeping through the trees and the window warm my face until Agnes took a sharp right down the gravel road toward the campsite.

"Looks like we got company." Agnes noticed another camper had pulled into the campsite near Ritchie Stinnett's cabin. "I'll drop you off at your camper, and then you get on out of here with Precious. Hank will bring her to me tonight."

"I thought you said you wanted to drop her off at home," I said. Agnes was making me wonder if she wasn't all there right now. She was talking in circles, being vague, and acting a wee bit nuts. "Fine. I'll do it."

I opened her car door and noticed Sue Ann Jaffarian was taking down the big tent Mason had made as headquarters for his hunt.

"Look, Sue Ann must be gathering all Mason's things. I bet she's super sad." A twinge of pain hit my stomach at the thought of losing a loved one to something like a strange and unexpected accident like a fall.

"Where you going?" Agnes had jerked open her door and yelled after me.

"I'm going to go say hello to her." I didn't want to, but I had no choice. I had to tell Hank about Agnes's odd behavior.

"Don't go near her!" Agnes called after me, but it was too late. Sue Ann was walking toward me. "She's illegally harvesting ginseng!"

"Illegally what?" I turned to look back at Agnes, who was walking as fast as she could toward me. Then I turned around when I heard a click.

Sue Ann Jaffarian pointed a handgun right at my head.

"Ritchie! Get out here now!" she screamed over to Ritchie's little cabin. "We got trouble!"

"Trouble" was all Ritchie needed to hear. I stood with my arms up, looking back and forth at Agnes and Sue Ann Jaffarian. Apparently, I'd totally missed what Agnes did to make Sue Ann mad.

Ritchie jerked open the door of his little cabin. He looked over at the three of us and reached inside the cabin, pulling out a shotgun.

EIGHTEEN

"What is going on here?" I tried to steady my voice as I looked at Sue Ann Jaffarian and Agnes Swift. The generation between them showed on their faces. "There's clearly something I'm missing. There's no need for a gun."

For some weird reason, I thought Sue Ann would listen to me and put the gun down, but that was positive thinking for sure.

"Lord have mercy on our souls," I whispered when I noticed Ritchie was taking all of Sue Ann's orders.

"Ritchie, has your butter slid off your biscuit?" Agnes asked.

I wished she'd not insulted him in this particular situation, but she kept going.

"When I see your mama and daddy at church on Sunday, I'm gonna tell them exactly what you did here. Holding me at gunpoint. I'd be ashamed." Agnes scolded him, not caring a bit about his shotgun pointed straight at her.

"Shut up. I'm so tired of listening to you talk and talk and talk." Sue Ann's attitude took a big turn. With one hand she bent down and picked up the rope from the information tent of Mason's that she had taken down, and kept the gun still pointed at us. "Tie them up." She threw the rope to Ritchie.

"She's right." Ritchie sounded a little beat up from Agnes yelling at him. He walked over to me with the rope and jerked my hands behind my back. "My mama and daddy will be disappointed if we get caught."

Sue Ann's face contorted in all sorts of ways that said she was annoyed. The huffing and puffing coming out of her was worse than a choo-choo train trying to travel up a steep hill.

Agnes and I stood before her with our hands tied behind our backs.

"We aren't getting caught. We will kill them and dispose of the bodies in the campfire. Go get it good and hot."

"Mae, you were asking about ginseng harvesting. Well, it seems Sue Ann can answer anything you need to know because she and Ritchie Stinnett have been illegally harvesting for the better part of five years, and that's why she killed Mason Cavanaugh." Agnes was about to get us shot right there. But she kept talking. "Hank has been busy working on this case for a few months, and he's so close to catching you. If you kill me, he'll kill himself hunting you down."

"If I'd known you were his beloved granny, I'd have killed you before I killed Dirk." Sue Ann's mouth twitched as she spat the nasty words from her mouth.

The campfire roared to life. Ritchie was throwing lighter fluid on it.

"You killed Dirk?" I gulped. "Mason?" I cried.

"Go on and tell her if you think you know so much." Sue Ann encouraged Agnes with a slight smile of defiance.

"Nah. I'll let you have that glory." Agnes wasn't backing down, and I normally admired that in her, but at the moment, I so wished she'd just apologize and beg for forgiveness.

So I did it.

"Listen, Agnes is eighty years old and a little senile, if you know what I mean." I jerked my head toward Agnes.

"Why, I am not," Agnes protested.

I spoke over her.

"Just let me get my campervan and drive me and her out of here. We won't look back. I don't know what you're doing, and I just learned about the ginseng so I have no knowledge of what's happening. I can even make Hank believe Agnes has lost her mind." I nodded, hoping Sue Ann would buy it, but she didn't.

"It's a little too late for negotiations. I mean, you're all tied up, and the fire is about ready to go." Sue Ann sighed and gave a resigned shrug.

"Why kill them?" Agnes kept poking Sue Ann, for sure going to get us killed before I could think of a way to get us out of here.

"Mason wasn't going to let it go. He was determined to turn me in when he saw me here." She laughed. "Only I had other plans for him."

"So the map of the campsite locations wasn't the map you were talking about?" I asked.

"It was the map. All those little Xs on it, those are where some ginseng fields are located and about to get taken out due to that stupid mayor of yours." Sue Ann had a steady gaze on me as she continued her awful actions. "He stole it from me because he was going to turn it in to

the cops. He told me not to show up to this year's John
Swift hunt because he knew it was perfect harvesting
season, and the treasure hunters always take the spotlight,
making it perfect for me to get my ginseng out and
overseas before anyone misses it."

I gulped.

"Are you telling me that you come here every year as a
treasure hunter but harvest the ginseng without a permit
and sell it?" I knew from what little research I'd done over
the past twenty-four hours about ginseng and Kentucky law
that it was very illegal to harvest and sell across state lines
without the appropriate permit.

"And here I thought you were a smart
businesswoman." She laughed. The chill between us grew.
I didn't like anyone, especially another woman, putting me
to the test. "Yes. That's exactly it. With Ritchie Stinnett
here to look in on the crops all year long, it was a perfect
business until Mason realized how little I was looking for
the treasure. That's when he caught on to my little side
hustle with Ritchie." She threw her head back and laughed.
"He thought I was sleeping with Ritchie. What a joke." She
rolled her eyes like Ritchie wasn't anywhere near her
dating league.

"You killed Mason because he was going to tell the police about your illegal business." I stressed *illegal*. "Dirk? Why? How?"

My head was having a hard time wrapping around the fact someone would kill two people over ginseng.

"Psst." Agnes kept trying to get my attention. When I looked at her, she gave me the shut-the-heck-up look, wrinkled her nose a few times, and looked down at herself with a few quick nods.

"That was perfect!" Sue Ann's voice echoed around the campsite. "You see, I came to the campsite the first night you were here so I could get a handle on what Mason knew and had up his sleeve. I knew he was going to go to the cops after the weekend hunt was over. When he thought I'd gone to the new campsite with my crew, I stayed in Ritchie's cabin so I could watch everything going on. I knew I was going to kill him, so when you were gone, I crept into your campervan and took the pearls after Ritchie told me how Mason begged her for them. It was a little insurance just in case we needed a killer." She beamed with pride in how smart she thought she was.

"That was perty good," Ritchie chimed in. I had to listen really hard to how his hillbilly accent changed words.

"I reckoned it was fine for me to tell Sue Ann how Dirk and Mason had fought so in case Merry Lizbeth didn't work out as a suspect, Dirk did."

"You disgust me." I spit on the ground near Ritchie's feet.

"Don't." Sue Ann put her hand out when he stalked toward me to do God knows what for me nearly spitting on him. "I'll let you shoot her with that big shotgun." She twisted her head from side to side. "Do you know what happens when you're shot by a shotgun?" She burst her free hand open. "Boom." Her eyes expanded, and she smiled.

"I like how you followed Mason to the Furnace and used the exact moment to push him off." Ritchie made it sound like some sort of fun game. It made my stomach curl.

Agnes continued to stand there with her chest all popped out. I would glance over at her, but she had no expression.

"It was perfect for you to lace Dirk's coffee with ginseng. I had no idea the caffeine from the coffee and the ginseng interact like that with the end result of a heart attack." Sue Ann's words hit me.

"The caffeine interacts with the ginseng to speed up the heart." My jaw dropped. "So Dirk did die of a heart attack, no thanks to you."

"We got rid of them. Investigation cleared that Mason had an unfortunate fall while Dirk had a massive heart attack, making everyone believe it was the curse of John Swift." She pretended to cry and gave a few sniffs to make it seem more real. "How sad. But now we have you two. I was hoping to get all this down and get the ginseng in my camper before anyone came to get your heap of junk."

Then all the conversations I'd had with Sue Ann over the past couple of days hit me like a ton of bricks. Sue Ann had told me about her relationship with Mason and how she couldn't've killed him. Then she referred to so many more secrets in the Daniel Boone National Forest than just the John Swift silver. She had to be talking about her little ginseng gig.

"The salad," I gasped, remembering when she gave me the map and the contents of her backpack fell out.

"Salad?" It was the first thing Agnes said since Sue Ann started confessing.

"Yea. When Sue Ann gave me the map to throw me off that she didn't kill Mason for some silly real treasure map that he claimed she stole from him." I snapped my eyes at her. "You knew I'd tell Hank how you broke up with Mason and how he stole the map from you."

"Girl's gotta cover her tracks." She winked, sending rage right through me. "Yes, it was a bag of ginseng that fell out along with some granola. How could you live here and not know about the ginseng?" She mocked me. "I honestly thought you were such a smart businesswoman."

"Far's ready." Ritchie Stinnett's accent made "fire" sound like "far."

"You take them over there, let them feel the heat on their skin so they know what it's gonna feel like to burn." Sue Ann really did enjoy torturing me and Agnes.

Ritchie laid his shotgun down on the ground and used one hand on each of us to jerk the rope, causing a little pain. Poor Agnes. She groaned out loud, making my heart drop to my toes. I truly didn't see any way out of this.

"Listen, I know people," I told Ritchie, hoping to strike a deal. "You won't go to jail. Just her."

"Any time now!" Agnes screamed and looked at me with big eyes.

"What? Any time now what?" I yelled back at her. "I'm trying to talk to Ritchie."

"I got it all!" Agnes's voice quivered.

"Got what?" Sue Ann put a hand out for Ritchie to stop dragging me and Agnes to the hot fire.

"Police! Rangers! Hold it right there." The voice boomed out of the woods right before hundreds of police fled out of the forest with headgear, bulletproof vests, goggles, and guns focused on Sue Ann Jaffarian and Ritchie Stinnett. Hank Sharp led the charge.

NINETEEN

"You should've seen him." Agnes Swift's eyes were glowing, and it wasn't from the campfire flames we were gathered around. "My grandson stormed in there just in time. We were 'bout to be burned at the stake."

"Well, I'll be," Dottie gushed. She was leaning forward in the chair with her elbows resting on her knees. She was enthralled with the story of how Hank had saved us from being murdered at the hands of Sue Ann Jaffarian and Ritchie Stinnett. "And you had on a wire?"

"I sure did. If it weren't for Mae and that map she gave me to make copies of, then we'd never have solved it." Agnes had fooled me when we were being held at gunpoint. She wasn't going senile. She was so with it she knew Hank had been working on the ginseng case.

In fact, later I'd found out Hank had held the fake news conference to throw Sue Ann and her group off, making them go about their business without trying to sneak around when they thought they might be suspects.

When I'd given her the map from Sue Ann, Agnes took it, thinking it might be something Hank would be interested in. He was! It just so happened to be the map where Sue Ann had marked all the hidden ginseng fields she and Ritchie had been illegally harvesting from, and that morning Hank and the rangers set out to find Sue Ann and her crew. When they realized she was at Ritchie's campsite still and I needed to get my campervan, Hank had wired Agnes and arranged for her to drive me there, knowing they were lurking in the woods.

"So you mean to tell me that Agnes tried every which way to get you to take Precious and your campervan out of there before she confronted them?" Dottie leaned back in the chair, laughing and clapping her hands. "Just like Mae to hang around."

"Mae West comes to the rescue again," I joked and looked over at Hank.

"You see this marshmallow?" He lifted up his stick from the fire. The marshmallow was on fire. "You were about to be burnt if it weren't for me."

"I thought for sure Mae was going to screw it up." Agnes didn't hold back. "She kept on talking and talking while I was trying to get Sue Ann's confession on the wire."

"Is that why you were pushing out your chest?" I started to laugh when I recalled her standing all funny like when I was trying to save our lives.

"It wasn't to show off my old tatas." Agnes *tsk*ed.

"Okay, when we start talking about my granny's women parts, it's time to call it a night." Hank stood up and put his hand out for me to take. "Let's go let the dogs out, and I'll walk you home."

"Show me how Agnes was all standing with her chest out." Dottie encouraged me to act like Agnes.

I pushed my chest out and walked away with Hank, leaving them both laughing and staring into the campfire.

"All joking aside, when you didn't leave the campsite like Agnes told you, my heart fell in my feet, and I almost called the raid off." Hank squeezed my hand. "You know, we found a single fingerprint on that pair of sparkly shoes you wore during the campfire story night."

"Sue Ann's." I gasped when I remembered she'd noticed my shoes and commented on the night I'd first seen her. "I bet she picked them up and looked at them when she broke into my campervan to take Mary Elizabeth's pearls."

"Yep. That's how I really pegged she was up to something, along with the map you gave Agnes from Sue Ann." Hank had just put all the pieces together. "Still, if anything had happened..." His voice trailed off.

The darkness had blanketed the campground, and since there weren't any lights but the full moon hanging overhead and the lightning bugs to guide us, I was glad he couldn't see my face or the tears that welled up on my eyelids.

"Mae, did you hear me?" Hank stopped and turned me toward him. He lifted his hands to my face. "I'm in love with you."

I blinked. A tear fell down my cheek. He used the pad of his thumb to wipe it away.

"I love you too," I whispered, sealing the words with a kiss.

RECIPES AND CLEANING HACKS FROM MAE
WEST AND THE WOMEN OF
NORMAL, KENTUCKY and HAPPY TRAILS
CAMPGROUND

Skillet Chicken Enchilada

Whether you decide to make this tasty dish over the campfire or in your RV or home oven, everyone is going to love it.

INGREDIENTS

Four cooked and shredded chicken breast

10 oz can enchilada sauce

½ chopped onion

3 TBS chopped garlic

Four corn tortillas, quartered

1 can black beans

¼ cup water

¼ cup of sour cream

1 TBS olive oil

1 package Mexican Cheese

DIRECTIONS

Cook over campfire:

Heat up the olive oil and add the onions and garlic.

Brown them for five minutes.

In a bowl mix: onions, garlic, enchilada sauce, sour cream, and water.

Fold in the tortillas, chicken, and beans.

When mixture is fully covered, add back into the skillet and warm over fire.

Add cheese on top and let it melt.

Cook on stove and in oven of the RV:

Preheat over to 500*

Heat up the olive oil and add the onions and garlic on stove.

Brown them for five minutes.

In a bowl mix: onions, garlic, enchilada sauce, sour cream, and water.

Fold in the tortillas, chicken, and beans.

When mixture is fully covered, add back into the skillet and warm it on the stove.

Add cheese on top and put it in the preheated oven for five minutes.

ENJOY!

RV HACK #1

This isn't really as much of a hack in cleaning, but a good hack for an acorn in case you ever need a whistle in case you get lost from your other hikers.

Acorn Whistle

Make the cap of an acorn into a whistle.

    1. Use the brown part on top of the acorn. Make sure it is not cracked or deformed.

    2. Grab the acorn cap in both of your hands between your thumb and index finger with the inside of the cap facing you.

    3. Put your thumbs up to near the top of the acorn. The sides of the knuckles of your thumbs should be touching each other.

    4. Position the acorn so that a triangle of it is showing out between the tops of your thumb-knuckles.

    5. Put your upper lip on the top of your thumb-knuckles. Make sure there's no air escaping your

bottom lip. This part will take the most practice but keep going!

6. Blow through your top lip right into the triangle that you had formed earlier.

Iron Skillet Hamburger Casserole

INGREDIENTS

1 pound(s) hamburger

1 medium onion, chopped

1/2 tsp chili powder

   1 can, ranch style beans

DIRECTIONS

Brown hamburger, onion and chili powder in a skillet over the camp fire until the hamburger is completely browned.

Add can of ranch style beans and continue to cook until beans are thoroughly heated.

ENJOY!

RV Hack #2

This isn't really a RV hack, but something great for your dog! There are a lot of animals that camp too. Your dog wants to be part of the action when you're outside so why not make them a nice little zipline?

Camping Carabiner, which is one of those clip keyrings.

Nylon Rope around 40 – 50 feet long

Two Spring Clasps

DIRECTIONS

Tie one end of the nylon rope to a spring clasp in a very tight knot on both ends.

Do the same to other end of the nylon rope with the opposite spring clasp.

Circle the rope around two trees or something as stable on each end.

Connect the spring clasp on the other side.

Connect the camping carabiner to the suspended nylon rope.

Connect your dog's harness to the camping carabiner.

Enjoy watching your fur baby hang outside with you too!

Iron Skillet French Toast

Ingredients

6 eggs lightly beaten

12 oz can evaporated skim milk

1/2 tsp ground cinnamon

1/2 cup brown sugar

6 slices of raisin bread with the crusts removed

2-3 tbsp diced butter

Maple syrup

Instructions:

Whisk together the eggs, evaporated milk, cinnamon and brown sugar, making sure the brown sugar completely dissolves.

Dip each piece of raisin bread into the egg mixture, coating completely, then lay in the skillet.

Repeat with until you cover the bottom of the skillet completely, then use the remaining pieces of bread to form a second layer.

Continue the layers until the bread is all gone.

Pour any remaining egg mixture on top and put the diced butter on top of that.

Bake 35-45 minutes in the grill or RV oven until the top is browned.

Keep Scrolling For A

Preview of the Scene of the Grind

Book One

A Killer Coffee Mystery

One

Drip, drip, drip.

There is something about coffee that brings people together. And they don't even have to like coffee. Is it the smell? Is it the comforting sound of the drip? I don't know. All I did know was that my new coffee shop in the touristy lake town of Honey Springs, Kentucky, The Bean Hive, was opened for business.

"Seven a.m.," I muttered after I'd glanced up at the clock and drew my eyes back out the front doors of the coffeehouse located in the best spot on the boardwalk that ran along Lake Honey Springs.

The boardwalk held fond memories for me since I used to spend my summers here with my Aunt Maxine. Maxi for short. For the past year my life was stalled in a little bit of what I'd call a fork in the road, so after hearing Aunt Maxi talk about all the revitalization of the boardwalk and not really knowing what to do, it sounded like a splendid idea to open a shop. At the time.

The annual Honey Festival was in a couple of days and all the vendors and the new shops on the boardwalk were holding a grand opening. I'd already had the coffeehouse ready to open since when I moved to Honey Springs a few weeks ago, I made it a point to no longer sit around resting on my laurels, so I opened the shop a few days early. Which might not've been the best business plan since my only customers had been a few stragglers here and there. Mainly construction workers who were working day and night to get the shops ready for the big festival.

The Bean Hive was located in the middle of the boardwalk, right across from the pier. It was a perfect spot and I was beyond thrilled with the exposed brick walls and wooden ceiling beams that I didn't have to touch. Luckily, Aunt Maxi owned the place. The rent was a little steep, but I'd watched a few DIY videos on YouTube to figure out how to make the necessary repairs for inspection. I couldn't be more pleased with the shiplap wall I'd created myself out of plywood painted white to make it look like real shiplap.

Instead of investing in a fancy menu or even menu boards that attached to the wall, I'd bought four large chalkboards that hung down from the ceiling over the L-shaped glass countertop.

The first chalkboard menu hung over the pie counter and listed the pies and cookies with their prices. The second menu hung over the tortes and quiches. The third menu before the L-shaped counter curved listed the breakfast casseroles and drinks. Over top the other counter the chalkboard listed lunch options, including soups, and catering information.

On each side of the counter was a drink stand. One was a coffee bar with six industrial thermoses with different blends of my specialty coffees as well as one filled with a decaffeinated blend, even though I clearly never understood the concept of that. But Aunt Maxi made sure I understood some people only drink the unleaded stuff. The coffee bar had everything you needed to take a coffee with you. Even an honor system where you could pay and go.

The drink bar on the opposite end of the counter was a tea bar. Hot tea, cold tea. There was a nice selection of gourmet teas and loose leaf teas along with cold teas. I'd even gotten a few antique tea pots from Wild and Whimsy

Antique shop, which happened to be the first shop on the boardwalk. If a customer came in and wanted a pot of hot tea, I could fix it for them or they could fix their own to their taste.

A few café tables dotted the inside along with two long window tables with stools butted up to them on each side of the front door. It was a perfect spot to sit, enjoy the beautiful Lake Honey Springs and sip on your favorite beverage.

Which just so happened to be where I was sitting this morning enjoying the view until I realized I'd been here since four a.m. to get the casseroles made and coffees brewed before the opening time of seven a.m. and no one was here.

"You did open a little early," I said to make myself feel better and hooked my finger in the mug of freshly brewed coffee.

Curling both hands around the mug, I leaned my hip up against the counter and took a sip. Even if no one showed up today, it was better than where I was a year ago. My chin lifted as the first rays of sunshine popped through the large front windows. I closed my eyes and let the breaking of the dawn fill my soul.

It was spring in Kentucky and the leaves were starting to get their deep green color back, filling in the tree line along the lake. A few fishing boats had trolled by since it was a no wake zone. Good fishing started around five a.m. around here and they were usually back by seven. At the far end of the pier was a marina with boat slips and a really neat little restaurant, The Watershed. It was probably the fanciest restaurant in Honey Springs.

With my mug in my hands, I decided to get a whiff of the fresh air.

The bell dinged over the front door when I opened it. Cool air swept in reminding me that spring in Kentucky was cold in the morning and hot in the afternoon. Dressing was always a problem, but with the few uniform pieces I'd picked to go with my black pants and sensible shoes I'd handle the change easily. Besides, the black apron with The Bean Hive logo was amazing and I'd gotten several of those.

Today I'd decided on the thin long-sleeved crew neck and had tied the apron over it.

Since there wasn't anyone in the coffeehouse, I'd decided to stroll to the right of the coffeehouse on the boardwalk and do a little window shopping, even though most of them weren't opening until the grand opening this weekend. I walked all the way to the end and looked as I made my way back, enjoying my cup of coffee and the morning sunrise as it dripped in many colors in the lake. It was funny how water could turn the orange and yellow rays different colors as it mirrored in the lake.

The shops were really coming along. All the shops were butted next to each other with a different awning to boast the name of the shop. Every few feet there were a couple of café tables where visitors could shop and stop to enjoy each other or just the view the boardwalk gave.

Wild and Whimsy was the first shop on the boardwalk. It was an eclectic shop of antiques and repurposed furniture. Beverly and Dan Teagarden were the owners. Their two grown children, Savannah and Melanie helped them run it. Instead of the regular shingled roof, Dan had paid extra to put on a rusty tin roof to go with the store's theme. They'd kept the awning a red color but without the name. The Wild and Whimsy sign dangled down from the awning.

Honey Comb Salon & Spa was located next and it was a fancy, for Honey Springs, salon. Alice Dee Spicer was the owner and from what I'd overheard through the gossip

line Alice had really gotten some new techniques from a
fancy school.

Next to Honey Comb Salon & Spa was the Buzz In
and Out Diner owned by James Farley. Honey Springs's
very first tattoo parlor, Odd Ink, was next to the diner. I
wasn't sure who owned that. In fact, I didn't know any of
the owners. It was all just idle gossip from Mae Belle and
Bunny's morning coffee run that kept me in the know.
They'd also said All About The Details, a new event center,
was going in next to the tattoo place along with a bridal
shop, Queen For The Day. Then there was me.

The Bean Hive.

The bait and tackle shop was the only shop that was on
the pier. It was perfect for the tourists who wanted to fish
for the day off the pier. They'd never closed like most of
the past shops since the lake always had fishermen. This
year was different.

The annual Honey Festival was also in a couple of
days, hence the grand opening of the shops, and it did bring
visitors far and wide to get a good sampling of our fine
Kentucky honey and festival activities. This year the town
council, of which my Aunt Maxi sits on the board, decided
to move the festival from Central Park in downtown Honey

Springs to the boardwalk. Vendors were going to be setting up along the boardwalk across from the shops. I was especially excited to purchase some fresh honey and honeycombs for the coffeehouse.

I'd yet to venture past my shop, but I did know there was some sort of clothing boutique, a knick-knack shop, a spa, a bar and at the very end was Crooked Cat Bookstore, which was an independent bookstore I'd spent many hours in during my summer visits. I fondly remembered a cat that snuggled up to me in the bean bag.

The smell of fresh coffee drifted out of the coffeehouse exactly how I'd envisioned it would. The warm scent filled me with joy where I wasn't sure I could have joy anymore.

When I opened the door to head back in, I smiled. The Bean Hive was a dream only a year ago and now a reality; I'd created it in my head and had worked hard to make the dream become real. After I filled my cup again, I walked back into the kitchen to check the casseroles I'd put in the oven for the afternoon lunch. I only cooked one thing a day for breakfast and lunch. I baked several things for the customers to enjoy and take home. The Bean Hive was a coffeehouse, not a restaurant, but we all know that food goes well with teas and coffee. It was my way of offering something for everyone.

Today's special was a sausage casserole that paired great with any flavor coffee or tea. Everything was made fresh, which made the coffeehouse fill with amazing, stomach rumbling aromas no one could refuse.

The bell over the door dinged. I rushed back in the dining area to greet the customer.

"I'm telling you something is wrong," Bunny Bowowski waddled into The Bean Hive with her brown pocketbook hung in the croak of her arm. "She didn't answer her phone all night last night."

"You know, I was by there just around eight o'clock and I did notice the strangest thing." Mae Belle Donovan stopped just inside the door and put her hand on Bunny's forearm. "You know those little plug-in candles that are in each one of her windows?"

"Do I?" Bunny rolled her eyes. "We downright got into a fight over them candles. In July of last year I told her that it was not Christmas and she needed to take them things down. In fact, it was hotter than a firecracker, not nary a thought of snow. She said it was decoration."

"Good morning, ladies." I greeted them like I'd done the past two mornings around this time.

According to Aunt Maxi, Bunny Bowowski and Mae Belle Donovan never left the house unless they were dressed in a dress, a shawl or coat (depending on the weather) and some sort of hat that sat on their heads like a bow as if it were completing the package.

They'd been friends for so long, they even resembled each other. Both had the exact same haircut, their grey hair was parted to the side and cut at chin length. They both carried a brown pocketbook that was perfectly held in the crook of their right elbow. Both were on the beautification committee. They came down every morning to get a look at the boardwalk to make sure everything was progressing right on schedule.

"Good morning to you." Bunny nodded and began to walk up to the counter. "Those are lovely daffodils."

"Thank you." I scooted them over to the right a little more so I could get a good view of my two customers. "Aren't they the most vibrant yellow you've ever seen?"

"Mmhmmm." Her brows formed a V.

"I got them at the farmer's market when I picked out my fresh produce and fruit. And this," I tapped the vase, very proud of my find, "I found this for one dollar at Wild and Whimsy."

"They do have some steals for an antique store." She rotated the clear hourglass vase that had a tin top and a round hole where the flowers went. She ran her finger along etched flowers in the glass. "You certainly got a bargain."

"Yes. I was very pleased." I pushed back a strand of my wavy black hair.

Wavy was a loose term for the springy naturally curly hair my head seemed to sprout as soon as water touched it. No matter how much I had it straightened, tried to straighten or even hide in a ponytail, a stray strand of hair sprung out from somewhere.

I glanced toward Mae Belle.

They weren't the spriest of women, but they certainly got around just fine.

"Hi do." Mae Belle gave a slight bow. "Something smells delicious."

"You are just in time for my country sausage casserole." I pointed to the glass pan I'd just taken out of the oven.

The melted cheese was still bubbling around the edges where it'd not cooled off yet.

"I'm letting it cool off so I can cut nice thick slices." I found it was best to let a dish cool for around ten minutes to not only set the casserole, but to let the flavors deepen and simmer within the ingredients. "If you'd like to have a cup of coffee while you wait for a slice of the casserole, I'd love to get you some."

"Oh, Roxanne, you do know us don't you." Bunny gave a theatrical wink. She pointed to one of the few café tables I had provided for the customers. "We'll go on over there."

I leaned way over the counter and whispered like I had a grand secret, "You can call me Roxy. All my friends do."

"Roxy with the amazing eyes." Bunny winked. "You do have beautiful blue eyes."

"Thank you." I smiled, grateful for the comment.

I poured two ceramic coffee mugs with The Bean Hive's own highlander grog and set them on a small round tray along with one of the silver cow cream pitchers I'd gotten on sale at Wild and Whimsy. Most of the china and silver I'd bought for The Bean Hive was from there, since the old things go great with the exposed brick walls, wood pallet furniture and big comfy chairs I'd used to decorate the shop, as well as the old tin signs and the chalkboard menus that hung above the counter.

"Roxy." A big smile curled up on her face. "Now that's a name with character."

"That's what I hear." I chuckled and excused myself where I retreated into the kitchen.

For the last year, I'd gotten up way before the rooster crowed, so to speak, which was about four a.m. around these parts. Only I hadn't been in these parts. Only recently had I moved back to Honey Springs. I'm not sure if it was to get away from the life I'd left behind due to my divorce or if I needed a little bit of familiarity or comfort. Regardless, I'm what I'd like to call a retired lawyer even at the young age of thirty. Retired because after my divorce, I hated lawyers. It was then that I'd listened to all that junk about following your passion. Doing what you love. Life is too short, yada-yada. One four a.m. morning, I couldn't sleep and fixed myself a cup of coffee. It was then and there that I decided I wanted to go to barista school and I've never looked back.

"The shops are looking great," I called over my shoulder on the way back to the kitchen to check the rest of the casseroles before I stuck the lunch ones in.

"We are pleased as peaches on how Cane Contractors has really stayed on schedule." I heard Bunny say after I walked through the door into the kitchen.

Cane Contractors. A lump formed in my throat at the sound of the name. It was very hard to swallow. I shook my head to make the thought go away.

"What on earth?" I looked at the convection oven with the morning sausage casseroles in it and noticed the digital buttons weren't lit up.

I hit the oven button and nothing. I opened the oven door. The casseroles were still running and lumpy. I stuck my hand in the oven and it was cold. Not a lick of heat.

"Great," I groaned and hurriedly took out a couple of the four casseroles I had in there and moved them to the other convection oven next to it where I crammed them in with the lunch quiches. "This is going to have to work." I gulped knowing it probably wasn't going to work since both of them required different cooking temperatures.

I headed back out to the shop and grabbed my cell phone out of the pocket of my apron and dialed my aunt Maxine.

"Aunt Maxi, I'm so glad you answered." My rapidly beating heart settled down after I'd heard the comforting sound of her voice.

"This better be good," the tone in her voice wasn't happiness. "I need my beauty sleep. I'm on the prowl ya know."

"Yeah, yeah." Prowl. My aunt was in her mid-sixties and widowed. Widowed at a young age too. But as far as I knew, she was happily single. "Listen, can you hurry down to the shop and grab some of the lunch quiches for me and put them in your oven to bake?" I asked.

"You didn't call a handyman yet?" She let me know that she'd warned me several times after I'd bought the place how the previous owner of the restaurant had undercooked food and eventually got shut down by the Health Department.

"No," I muttered, knowing I really should've listened to her but the cost was something I wasn't able to afford right now. "I was trying to wait until this first week was open and then I'd hire one."

"I'm going to say I told you so, just because I can say I told you so and you won't give no sass back. I told you so," she said in a playful voice. "I'll be right over."

"Thank you so much. I love you and I know you love me." A sigh of relief escaped me.

There weren't too many times Aunt Maxi didn't save me. In fact, the reason I'd come back to Honey Springs was due to her. I love my mom but she seemed to hover around me when I'd gone home to Lexington after my divorce. Aunt Maxi had lived in Honey Springs all her life and she was my dad's sister. Unfortunately, he'd died of cancer years ago. I'd spend summers here with Aunt Maxi and the cozy town had become a second home to me.

I loved the small shops scattered throughout the town. But the boardwalk and pier were my favorite spots in Honey Springs. Aunt Maxi owned a few rental properties, The Bean Hive being one as well as Crooked Cat Bookstore plus a couple residential places. Unfortunately for me, she didn't have any houses available, so I bought a pretty run-down cabin alongside the lake and only a four-minute bike ride from the coffeehouse.

It was a perfect place to live, but needed a few upgrades. Still, it was mine and I loved every part of it, even the broken ones.

"Are you ladies ready for your slice of country sausage casserole?" I asked and sliced into the warm casserole, plating two nice sized pieces on two lattice, milk glass plates. "Here you go." I set a plate down in front of each of them.

"This looks amazing, Roxy." Bunny leaned over the plate. She closed her eyes and inhaled. "And smells delicious."

There was nothing as satisfying to me as seeing someone who enjoyed something I'd made with my hands.

"Thank you." I took a step back and put my hands in a prayer position up in front of my face. "I'm honored. I hope you enjoy the taste too."

"I'm sure we will," she said.

Mae Belle didn't have to say anything. She'd already dug in and was on her third bite.

I walked over to the door not only to see if Aunt Maxi was on her way, but to see if there was anyone walking along the boardwalk who I could offer a free coffee to. Even if some of the construction workers were employed by Cane, there was a lot of construction going on and even they had to eat or at least warm up with a coffee. My eyes scanned the workers to make sure I didn't see anyone I knew from my past summers here. There was a bit of satisfaction and a bit of sadness when I didn't recognize any of them. It was probably a good thing.

"You've outdone yourself with this one," Mae Belle called from behind me and forced me to come back out of my memories that were good and bad.

"Thank you so much." I stared down the boardwalk where a tall, lean man with a yellow hardhat on was standing next to the new beauty salon and spa.

He had a set of plans rolled out in front of him. A couple of men on each side of him were looking at the plans. They nodded and spoke with each other. The early morning chill had yet to give way to the spring afternoon weather. I knew the spa was going to open along with most of the other shops before the annual spring Honey Festival in hopes that'd bring the tourists we needed to revitalize the sleepy town. That was one of the reasons I'd moved back. The fond memories of lazy days spent on the pier and watching all the people going in and out of the shops outweighed the only bad memory I'd had. Those days had been long gone and now I was going to do my part to help bring it back.

Not only did the Honey Springs economy need it, I needed it to help restore my soul.

"Are you two okay?" I asked on my way back to the counter.

They nodded and went back to discussing their friend who apparently hadn't shown up for a meeting or something.

I grabbed a thermos that could hold six cups of coffee and stuck it under the Bunn Industrial coffee maker to fill. While it filled up, I grabbed a few to-go cups. I ran a finger over the cute The Bean Hive logo I'd designed. It was fun to see the bee that had a coffee bean for a body come to life on the materials I'd had printed for merchandise as well as on marketing materials.

The bell over the door dinged and I looked up.

"Alexis Roarke," Bunny greeted the petite blonde. "We were just discussing where you've been."

"You have," Alexis Roarke wore her blond hair in a conservative nature with a bob cut just beneath her ears and straight across bangs. She had on pair of tennis shoes, khakis, and a pull over hoodie with the Honey Springs logo on it.

"I even went by your house and your *decorative* candles weren't even lit up." Mae Belle eyed her suspiciously.

"Why, Mae Belle Donovan," Alexis drew her hands up to her chest. "You do care about me."

"Of course, we do." Bunny pushed back the only extra chair at their café table. "Sit." She patted the seat. "Where have you been?"

Alexis waved her off and was content standing next to the table.

"I don't have time to sit. I've got to open the shop. Maxine Bloom is at it again," she said my aunt's name with exhaustion. "Raising the rent on the bookstore. I'm gonna have to stop volunteering at the Pet Palace."

"Why? Because you volunteer with Maxine?" Bunny asked and sipped on her coffee.

"No. So I can keep the bookstore open an extra day. I close early on Fridays so I can go volunteer. No more." She shook her head. She pointed at me and shook her finger. "I hear you are Maxine's niece."

"You hear right." I offered a warm smile in hopes she didn't hold it against me that my aunt Maxine was her landlord. "Did I also hear you say that you are the owner of Crooked Cat Bookstore?"

"I am." Her eyes narrowed as though she was sizing me up.

"I have fond memories of your bookstore when I used to come visit during the summer." A happy sigh escaped me. "I remember sitting in that big purple bean bag that was in the front window next to the cat tree. You had that little grey cat and that amazing banned book section."

"I'll be. I remember your eyes." A smile formed and reached her eyes. They twinkled as though the memory was bright. "That's when Maxine and I got along. She'd bring you in there while she was doing her property rounds and tell you to read books. I knew I was watching you."

"I believe my love of reading stems from you and all the time I spent in your store." I pointed to the coffee maker. "Can I get you a cup of coffee? On the house."

"Ours wasn't," Mae Belle grumbled under her breath.

"I'd love one to go. And give me one of them cake doughnuts." She pulled her chin to the side, and tilted her eyes over her shoulder as she enjoyed the look on Mae Belle's face.

With the to-go cup of coffee and The Bean Hive bag filled with a doughnut, she bid her friends goodbye.

"I'll see y'all at the town council meeting tomorrow. I've got a few things to say about this zoning thing and Maxine Bloom." She skirted out of the shop.

Mae Belle and Bunny put their heads together and both tried to whisper above the other. I figured it was a good time to take the workers the coffee.

"I'll be right back. I'm going to run some coffee down to the workers." I held the thermos up along with the cups.

The sun was popping up over the trees that stood along the lake like soldiers and filtered over the calm water of the lake. There were a couple of small bass boats running side-by-side with a couple of men in them, probably looking for a good inlet to bass fish.

The wood boards of the boardwalk groaned underneath each step I took as I got closer to the group of men.

"Good morning," I greeted them. "I'm Roxanne Bloom, owner of The Bean Hive." I gestured toward the coffee shop. "I've made all this coffee and only a few customers have come in." I left out the fact that I'd only had the same two customers all week long. "And I'd hate to see this fresh coffee go to waste, so I thought I'd bring it to y'all."

"That's mighty nice of you." The tall man grinned from under the hardhat. He kept his eyes on the thermos.

One of the men took the cups out of my hand while another one took the thermos.

"We appreciate that, don't we boys?" The man's deep voice echoed off the limestone banks of the lake. The glare of the sun reflecting off the lake made it difficult to see his face.

The men thanked me.

"If y'all get hungry, I also serve food." I smiled and clasped my hands in front of me. I was definitely trying to use the old saying that a way to a man's heart was through his stomach. Not that I was trying to get into any of their hearts, I wasn't, but I was trying to get to their stomachs and their wallets. "Enjoy."

"We will. And we will return your thermos," the man said before he went back to pointing out things about the spa.

It was my cue to head on back. They had work to do and so did I.

"Hello, honey." Aunt Maxi was leaning her bike up against the outside of the shop. She pulled off her knit cap. She tucked the hat in the purse that was strapped across her body and pulled out a can of hairspray. She raked her hand upward through her hair and used her other hand to spray it to high heaven. "You know, you need to get a bike rack."

"I do need a bike rack, but I also need to get a new oven or have this one looked at." I opened the door for her and let her walk in before me. "New hair color since yesterday?"

She gave the newly blond-colored hair another good spray before she stuck the can back in her purse and started toward the door.

"Alice Dee down at the Honey Comb says it's all the rage. Makes me feel young as a whippersnapper." She turned to me. The morning sun sprinkled down upon her.

I shook my head and realized having her bike up against the coffeehouse was probably not a good place for it to lean in case someone tripped over it.

Most of the community rode bikes everywhere since Honey Springs was a small, compact town that took pride in their landscape and Kentucky bluegrass that made the entire town look like a fancy landscape painting.

"You look a little like Phyllis Diller." And it wasn't just the hair. Aunt Maxi had put on a little too much makeup

"Well, well. If it's not Maxine Bloom." Bunny Bowowski didn't seem all that happy to see Aunt Maxi. "And with a new hairdo."

"You'll serve just about anybody." Aunt Maxi curled her nose at me.

"You two know each other?" I asked, hoping to bring a little peace between us.

"Know her?" Bunny scoffed. "She's been down at the Moose trying to get her claws into Floyd, my man."

"Don't flatter yourself, Bunny. I want a man that can walk without stopping every two feet so he can get his footing up under him so he don't fall." Aunt Maxi drew her chin in the air and looked down her nose. "Besides, that's not what's got you all worked up."

"Aunt Maxi is why I've come to Honey Springs." I patted my aunt on the back. "I used to come here when I was a child and spent many summers here. Right here in this very spot when it was the diner. I loved being here so much, that I decided to move here and open The Bean Hive."

I hoped that their mutual like for me would at least bring them together. The last thing I needed was my only two paying customers to boycott me because of Aunt Maxi.

"We will see you tomorrow, Roxy." Bunny stood up and motioned for Mae Belle to follow. "We've got committee stuff to do."

The three women gave each other the Baptist nod where they didn't wish ill-will but not necessarily success. The southern woman's way around good manners.

"Glad they're gone." Aunt Maxi spouted out and walked to the back of the shop. She put her hands on her hips and looked around. "This looks good," she said in approval. "Many customers?"

"Nope, you just ran off the only two I've had since I opened." I gave her a wry look. "Cup of coffee?"

"I can't. I've got to get your casseroles and head to a meeting. It's hard being a councilwoman." Aunt Maxi had held the office for over thirty years and was very proud of it. "That's why old Bunny is all mad. She and her group of cronies think that just because we are in craft group together that I'll just let them do whatever they want regarding the festivals and the beautification committee."

Apparently Aunt Maxi didn't agree on something in their meeting. Didn't surprise me. Aunt Maxi wasn't one to go along with the crowd when she was passionate about something. There were two things I knew not to get into with others: Politics and religion. Around here both were just as important as a new born baby, wedding, or a funeral. "They aren't too worried about whatever it is that you've made them mad about. They are worried about one of their friends."

"Who?" Aunt Maxi perked up and walked on my heels on our way back to the kitchen.

"I don't know. I can't remember her name. She actually came in." I grabbed the two lunch quiches I'd taken out of the oven earlier and wrapped them in tinfoil, pinching the sides as tight as I could. "She owns Crooked Cat."

"Alexis Roarke." Aunt Maxi groaned.

I laughed and stacked the two quiches. "She said that you two are fond of each other."

"Don't get me started on her because I don't come with brakes." Aunt Maxi picked up the quiches. "You know those left-over doughnuts you gave me yesterday?"

"Yes. What about them?" I asked.

"I took them to her last night. Sort of a peace offering," Aunt Maxi said. "She was just fine. So there's no need to worry about her. Those women love to worry. If they aren't gossiping or worried about someone, they're dead."

"They were happy to see her and that she was okay." I was just about to ask her about Alexis's claim that Aunt Maxi was going to raise the rent, but the bell over the shop door dinged, alerting me that someone had come in.

Aunt Maxi and I looked.

"Good morning, Maxine." The man I'd taken coffee to took off his hardhat with his left hand, his right gripped the thermos.

"Good to see you." Aunt Maxi's joy of seeing the man was evident all over her face. Even her eyes tipped up in the corners with giddiness.

"I wanted to thank you for the coffee. My men appreciate your kindness." His features were familiar. His big brown eyes were warm and matched the tender smile.

"I'm glad to see the two of you have mended ways. You know I believe everything happens for a reason." Aunt Maxi walked over to the door as she recited her favorite saying. "I'll have these back to you in a couple of hours. See you later, Patrick."

Patrick? I took a deeper look at the man standing in front of me. Patrick Cane? I looked a little deeper. Patrick Cane.

My heart sank.

RECIPES AND CLEANING HACKS FROM MAE WEST AND THE WOMEN OF NORMAL, KENTUCKY and HAPPY TRAILS CAMPGROUND

Skillet Chicken Enchilada

Whether you decide to make this tasty dish over the campfire or in your RV or home oven, everyone is going to love it.

INGREDIENTS

Four cooked and shredded chicken breast

10 oz can enchilada sauce

½ chopped onion

3 TBS chopped garlic

Four corn tortillas, quartered

1 can black beans

¼ cup water

¼ cup of sour cream

1 TBS olive oil

1 package Mexican Cheese

DIRECTIONS

Cook over campfire:

Heat up the olive oil and add the onions and garlic.

Brown them for five minutes.

In a bowl mix: onions, garlic, enchilada sauce, sour cream, and water.

Fold in the tortillas, chicken, and beans.

When mixture is fully covered, add back into the skillet and warm over fire.

Add cheese on top and let it melt.

Cook on stove and in oven of the RV:

Preheat over to 500*

Heat up the olive oil and add the onions and garlic on stove.

Brown them for five minutes.

In a bowl mix: onions, garlic, enchilada sauce, sour cream, and water.

Fold in the tortillas, chicken, and beans.

When mixture is fully covered, add back into the skillet and warm it on the stove.

Add cheese on top and put it in the preheated oven for five minutes.

ENJOY!

RV HACK #1

This isn't really as much of a hack in cleaning, but a good hack for an acorn in case you ever need a whistle in case you get lost from your other hikers.

Acorn Whistle

Make the cap of an acorn into a whistle.

7. Use the brown part on top of the acorn. Make sure it is not cracked or deformed.

8. Grab the acorn cap in both of your hands between your thumb and index finger with the inside of the cap facing you.

9. Put your thumbs up to near the top of the acorn. The sides of the knuckles of your thumbs should be touching each other.

10. Position the acorn so that a triangle of it is showing out between the tops of your thumb-knuckles.

11. Put your upper lip on the top of your thumb-knuckles. Make sure there's no air escaping

your bottom lip. This part will take the most practice but keep going!

12. Blow through your top lip right into the triangle that you had formed earlier.

Iron Skillet Hamburger Casserole

INGREDIENTS

1 pound(s) hamburger

1 medium onion, chopped

1/2 tsp chili powder

2 can, ranch style beans

DIRECTIONS

Brown hamburger, onion and chili powder in a skillet over the camp fire until the hamburger is completely browned.

Add can of ranch style beans and continue to cook until beans are thoroughly heated.

ENJOY!

RV Hack #2

This isn't really a RV hack, but something great for your dog! There are a lot of animals that camp too. Your dog wants to be part of the action when you're outside so why not make them a nice little zipline?

Camping Carabiner, which is one of those clip keyrings.

Nylon Rope around 40 – 50 feet long

Two Spring Clasps

DIRECTIONS

Tie one end of the nylon rope to a spring clasp in a very tight knot on both ends.

Do the same to other end of the nylon rope with the opposite spring clasp.

Circle the rope around two trees or something as stable on each end.

Connect the spring clasp on the other side.

Connect the camping carabiner to the suspended nylon rope.

Connect your dog's harness to the camping carabiner.

Enjoy watching your fur baby hang outside with you too!

Iron Skillet French Toast

Ingredients

 6 eggs lightly beaten

 12 oz can evaporated skim milk

 1/2 tsp ground cinnamon

 1/2 cup brown sugar

 6 slices of raisin bread with the crusts removed

 2-3 tbsp diced butter

 Maple syrup

Instructions:

Whisk together the eggs, evaporated milk, cinnamon and brown sugar, making sure the brown sugar completely dissolves.

Dip each piece of raisin bread into the egg mixture, coating completely, then lay in the skillet.

Repeat with until you cover the bottom of the skillet completely, then use the remaining pieces of bread to form a second layer.

Continue the layers until the bread is all gone.

Pour any remaining egg mixture on top and put the diced butter on top of that.

Bake 35-45 minutes in the grill or RV oven until the top is browned.

About the Author

Tonya has written over 55 novels and 4 novellas, all of which have graced numerous bestseller lists including USA Today. *Best known for stories charged with emotion and humor and filled with flawed characters, her novels have garnered reader praise and glowing critical reviews. She lives with her husband and a very spoiled rescue cat, Ro-Ro, and grew up in the small southern Kentucky town of Nicholasville. Now that her four boys are grown men, Tonya writes full time.*

Visit Tonya:

Facebook at Author Tonya Kappes

https://www.facebook.com/authortonyakappes

Kappes Krew Street Team

https://www.facebook.com/groups/208579765929709/

Webpage

tonyakappes.com

Goodreads

https://www.goodreads.com/author/show/4423580.Tony
a_Kappes

Twitter

https://twitter.com/tonyakappes11

Pinterest

https://www.pinterest.com/tonyakappes/

For weekly updates and contests, sign up for Coffee Chat
with Tonya newsletter via her website or Facebook.

Also by Tonya Kappes

GET WITCH or DIE TRYING

A Laurel London Mystery Series
CHECKERED CRIME
CHECKERED PAST
CHECKERED THIEF

A Divorced Diva Beading Mystery Series
A BEAD OF DOUBT SHORT STORY
STRUNG OUT TO DIE
CRIMPED TO DEATH

Olivia Davis Paranormal Mystery Series
SPLITSVILLE.COM
COLOR ME LOVE (novella)
COLOR ME A CRIME

Grandberry Falls Series
THE LADYBUG JINX
HAPPY NEW LIFE
A SUPERSTITIOUS CHRISTMAS (novella)
NEVER TELL YOUR DREAMS

Bluegrass Romance Series
GROOMING MR. RIGHT
TAMING MR. RIGHT

Women's Fiction
CARPE BREAD 'EM

Young Adult
TAG... YOU'RE IT

Copyright